WHEN THE TIME COMES

By

JERRY D. YOUNG

Creative Texts Edition

Published by

CREATIVE TEXTS PUBLISHERS

BARTO, PA

www.creativetexts.com

COVER PHOTO USED BY LICENSE

CREDIT: Nick Mealey

PROLOGUE

"What the heck?" asked the brakeman as he looked under the railroad car carrying liquefied petroleum gas. "That's not right." He squatted down and studied the small device on the unloading valve.

He stood and looked down the line of cars. Fifteen of them. He keyed the radio mike as he started to run back toward the engine, noting that every car had one of the devices. "Call 911!"

It was all he managed to get out before, in the matter of eleven seconds, all fifteen devices activated. Fifteen valves opened, and LPG began to splash down onto the ground. Before the last valve was open the brakeman slipped and fell, inhaling some of the liquid and freezing his lungs in an instant.

The liquid rolled down the slope, right into Chicago, barely giving off any vapors. The air temperature was just below freezing, and the LPG made it even colder. The LPG wouldn't detonate until enough vapors came off the liquid and mixed with the air in the correct concentration for a spark, of any kind, to ignite it.

Hundreds would die just from the liquid and the initial vapors as they spread rapidly in that area of the city before that combination came together, but when it did, hundreds of thousands more would suffer the consequences of the largest explosion of LPG ever witnessed.

"This is Kellie Manson reporting," said the video reporter on her first major assignment for the upstart Stringer News Network.

“We are here waiting for the official City of Chicago, State of Illinois, and DHS response to the internet spread threat of a coming major terror attack here in the city.

“Speculation, and it is only speculation, is that a re-vitalized al-Qaida terror organization is behind... Wait. Here come the authorities to speak.”

Kellie turned to watch, along with dozens of other reporters from several mediums, as the Mayor of Chicago began to speak. But she didn’t watch for long. The sound of a huge explosion hurt everyone’s ears, and then a shock wave rocked them on their feet.

All eyes turned in the direction of the huge smoke cloud that was billowing upward not too far away. Other, much smaller explosions were heard, though none produced such a shock wave as the first one.

CHAPTER ONE

"This is Kellie Manson reporting for Stringer News Network."

Stringer News Network was new, but they had the best state of the art equipment available. They were the first ground news team to reach the site of the explosion. Only two news helicopters were in the air, and from the chatter on the air-band scanners, they were being warned away from the area.

"Behind me you see the massive destruction wrought by the release and subsequent detonation of Liquefied Petroleum Gas. Estimated from what we could see of the ripped and torn railroad cars, there were at least twelve, and perhaps as many as twenty. But the gas... actually, the liquid, was released before the explosion.

"If I remember my chemistry, LPG is stored in liquid form and used as a gas through a regulator. The liquid would not explode, only the gas vapors coming off of it, slowly, due to the cold temperatures. Once the vapors mix with enough oxygen in the atmosphere, any sort of spark will cause the gas to explode, which will then disperse the liquid, heat it, and turn it into more gas which will also explode.

"This is the evidence I am seeing. As we get additional information we will broadcast it. This is Kellie Manson reporting for Stringer News Network. Back to the studio."

Kellie waited for Justin's clear signal before she looked away from the camera. She turned and looked at the smoky haze still hovering over the area of destruction. Kellie looked up at one of the helicopters flying over the area and shook her head. That would have been a much better vantage point. But SNN only had a few choppers and none of them were in Chicago. On the way, but not there.

"Let's pack it up and get back on the road," Marcy Neighbors, Kellie's producer, said. "Home base has a lead on another story. Roy will put someone back out here if needed."

"But this is..." Kellie began to protest.

"We go where they tell us, Kellie," Marcy said gently. "There's always another story to cover. Usually bigger and more impressive."

"But this is..." Kellie let her words trail away again. She had a gut feeling about this story. That it wasn't over. Not by a long shot. But Marcy had agreed to take a chance with her and Kellie wasn't going to let her down. It had been sheer luck the team was in Chicago when the event happened, on the way from New York for Los Angeles with a full mobile crew to set up another presence for the network on the west coast.

But when the gear was packed and everyone was standing around, ready to board the vehicles, Marcy held up her hand. She was talking on her cell phone. Kellie watched Marcy intently. She'd only known her for a few weeks, but had already learned to read Marcy fairly well. And right now, Marcy was a wide open book. Something big was happening.

"What is it, Marcy?" Kellie asked as soon as Marcy put away her phone and turned toward the group.

"Another internet report," Marcy said, walking closer and raising her voice just enough for the crew to hear. She didn't want to give away anything to the other news crews still on the scene.

"A threat against St. Louis. Same circumstances as before. No demands, just that something big will happen in St. Louis within three days. So saddle up, people. We're going to St.

Louis. They are diverting the helicopter there so we should have some eyes in the sky."

There was a little murmuring, but the crew was a good one. Handpicked from dozens of applicants when Stringer News Network began the hiring process in New York, many of them had been personally invited to apply by some of the movers and shakers at SNN.

Kellie was the greenest, and knew it. She was making a great effort to learn everything she could from every person on the crew, no matter their actual job. She'd decided early on that knowing the whole process was much better than just being the talking head in a video report.

If she could understand what the others needed from her to get the best report out possible, then she'd be a big step ahead. She was determined to not be just a talking head. She wanted to report the news, accurately and completely.

Marcy crooked a finger at Kellie as the others boarded their assigned vehicles. Kellie walked over. "Find out what you can online about something called rice blast."

"This have something to do with what is going on?"

"Don't know. It came up in some basic research home base is doing. Might be, might not be, but I want us in on it if it is."

"I'm on it," Kellie said. She hefted her computer case and jump bag into position so she could board the custom bus that carried the bulk of the crew. The others, in teams of two or three, drove the other vehicles needed to put a signal on the satellite network, or even locally on air if it might be required.

The bus was equipped with extensive communications systems, including long range radios and high speed, high reliability satellite internet connections.

Kellie settled herself, got a bottle of water and a ration bar from her jump bag and took out her computer. A few moments later, as the bus trembled slightly when it pulled away from the scene of devastation in Chicago, Kellie muttered, “What the hey is rice blast? Sounds like a new power drink.”

It didn’t take Kellie long to find out what she was looking for, and it wasn’t a new power drink. Far from it. What she learned sent a chill down her back when she realized the potential problems if the rice blast was, in fact, related to the terrorist attacks.

But Kellie didn’t stop with rice blast. The information led her to other subjects, each new one just as worrisome as the last. By the time they arrived at the hotel that had been booked for their stay, Kellie had more than enough information to take to Marcy and explain the theory she had come up with.

“Ah, Kellie! Honey! You’ve done a good job researching, but this is a little early to be proposing such a theory, isn’t it?”

“But it fits,” Kellie insisted quietly.

“Fits what?” Marcy asked. “A propane explosion in Chicago and a threat for something in St. Louis. I’m not seeing any connections yet. And you have a terrorist plan all laid out.”

“It does sound a bit farfetched when you put it that way,” Kellie sighed. “It all just seemed to fall into place while I was doing the research. I guess I am short on motive, method, and even probable responsible party.”

"Exactly," Marcy said. "But I like your thoroughness. Keep thinking things through and we might just get a scoop. But SNN is adamant about speculation without supporting facts. At least speculation that isn't labeled as such. But factual presentations are always best. And you're good with facts. Now, I want to get something real to eat, a bath, and some sleep. Johnny will notify us if anything comes up from home base or anywhere else, for that matter."

Kellie nodded. She could use a bite to eat, herself. And some rest. She'd learned to rest when she could, because stories often ran on their own timeline, with no consideration for the needs of human reporters.

But Kellie didn't sleep long. The information she'd found was still bothering her. So she did a little more online research, and then let her fingers do some walking in the Yellow Pages. There were several Universities and Colleges around the St. Louis area. And some of them had Agricultural programs.

It was too late to do anything else at the moment, so Kellie joined the crew for a late supper and strategy and planning meeting. She had her micro recorder going, and was taking notes, never quite confident of electronics working when needed.

At the end of the meeting, Kellie brought up the subject she'd been waiting to approach Marcy with. "Marcy, how about some local color and a look into the local preparedness situation?"

"Read my mind," Marcy chuckled. "That was the assignment I planned to give you in the morning. I want to know everything about the local disaster preparedness capabilities."

Kellie smiled. "Most excellent."

CHAPTER TWO

"This is Kellie Manson reporting for Stringer News Network."

Kellie held the microphone out slightly and turned to address the man standing beside her. "In light of the internet announcement of a possible attack on St. Louis, on the order of the one in Chicago, how ready is the city to handle such an event?"

Kellie led the conversation, and a dozen more, all through the day as Marcy and the researchers came up with additional people for her to interview. She was patient, and waited until there was a pause with no new contact to interview.

"Marcy," Kellie said, "How about I take a portable and do a little work on my own?"

Marcy's eyes widened. "On your own? I thought you preferred to be unencumbered and let the pros do their own thing."

"Mostly I do," Kellie said. "Yes. But I have a couple of ideas I want to follow up on. And just get some practice with the equipment. Just in case."

"Well, as long as you stay in touch and don't break anything."

"Oh, I'm always careful," Kellie said with a laugh. "Haven't fallen down in quite a while."

Marcy smiled. "I was taking about the equipment."

Both women laughed. Kellie hurried away to talk to Justin about using one of the lighter, more portable, one person cameras. He gladly led her through the process again. It wasn't the first time she'd asked for help and some training.

He thought it was a good trait for a reporter to have. Understanding the limitations and the strengths of the video medium.

As the crew got ready to go back to the hotel, Kellie sat in the small, unmarked van that was one of the vehicles used for miscellaneous tasks, mostly going after food and drinks when on location. She marked a map with some locations after getting phone directions and permission to interview three people at different agriculture educational facilities.

The first interview was pretty much a bust, in Kellie's opinion. The woman was more interested in Kellie than in the questions Kellie was asking.

The second wasn't much better. The elderly professor went off on tangent more than he stayed on track. With a sigh, Kellie headed for the third appointment. Her shoulder was hurting from toting the camera to and from the locations and setting it up and adjusting it on the tripod for the interviews.

Not too hopeful this time, Kellie was pleased to see a younger man, and a more mature woman, in the office she'd been directed to when she arrived at the building.

The man quickly stepped forward and helped Kellie get the camera bag off her shoulder and on the table.

"You're new," said the woman, after introductions. She was Imelda Montez, and the man was Hadley Robertson. "You think SNN will be able to compete?"

"I think so," Kellie said diplomatically. "We are trying to take a fresh approach to reporting the news. More accurate and thorough than some off the cuff description of fair and balanced. We feel that the viewer should be provided with the information available and allowed to make their own decisions as to what it means."

"That's a fresh approach, all right," replied Hadley. He was studying the camera. "Wow. Nice piece of equipment. Where do you want Imelda and I'll make myself scarce."

Kellie lifted an eyebrow.

"Give me a minute," Imelda said with a smile. She turned to Hadley. "Come on, Hadley. You have to get over this camera shyness. You are an up and comer. Going to be doing big things in Agriculture in the coming years. You are going to have to be prepared to face cameras and reporters."

Kellie saw Hadley sigh. "But you're the expert..."

"No longer," Imelda replied. "You know as much as I do, now, and are in the process of surpassing everything I dreamed of doing. You'll be a great replacement for me beginning next year when I retire. So, I may add a bit here and there, but you do the interview."

Hadley looked around at Kellie. "I guess I need to ask, where do you need me?"

"There at the desk would be fine," Kellie replied.

She'd set up the camera with the intention to do the interview from behind it, since the first two with her on camera hadn't gone that well.

"I just want to ask some questions. It relates to a story I might be doing in the future. I need background information, and then information on a couple of food plant diseases."

"Came to the right place," Imelda said. She'd taken a seat near Hadley, but off camera. Kellie made a quick adjustment to bring her into the scene.

"Hadley here is one of the leading experts on plant diseases and ways to combat them."

Kellie looked at Hadley. "Oh?"

Looking a bit uncomfortable, Hadley began to list his qualifications. Kellie almost stopped him, but he was relaxing slightly, so she let him talk.

She started slightly when he finished up with, "And I suppose my specialty is, and will be, fungal diseases of food plants, since they have one of the greatest possible impacts on both the qualitative and the quantitative production of staple foods for the whole world. Not to mention the financial impacts."

"Fungal diseases?" Kellie asked, just a bit tense now herself. "Rice blast?"

Hadley's eyes widened slightly. "Why, yes. Rice blast. Soybean rust, stem rust in wheat, corn smut in maize, and late blight in potatoes Some others.

"Outside of my field, but highly important, is the role fungi play in bee colony collapse disorder. The lack of bees to pollinate crops is an issue in itself."

"I've done a little research..." Kellie said.

All of Hadley's nervousness was gone now as he launched into a highly informative presentation about the diseases. Kellie was kept busy with the camera when Hadley began to get up and show various charts, pictures, samples, exhibits, examples, and projected computer images.

When Hadley ran down, with a sudden shy, "Sorry. I get carried away, sometimes."

"All just what I was wanting. I have a couple of questions that might seem a bit strange, but I ask you to give your best opinion... Would, in your opinion, these diseases be usable as a weapon of mass destruction? In the form of reducing the supplies of basic food staples for the US population? In causing starvation?"

Hadley didn't look surprised. Neither did Imelda. "Very much so. It is a real fear of mine. The impacts are so far reaching... Not just the US. If the diseases were weaponized and released into the food supply, it would affect the entire world population. Billions of deaths."

Kellie felt herself blanch and that chill go down her back again. "Did you say billions? With a B?"

Hadley nodded. "I'd say even as much as ninety percent of the earth's population. In excess of six billion people dead, from direct and indirect effects of the diseases."

"Indirect? Other than starvation?" Kellie asked. She hadn't thought about that.

"Oh, yes. Perhaps the majority of deaths would be indirect effects. Widespread riots over available food supplies. Wars between nations over that same food. Border clashes as people in areas hardest hit try to get to places that still have food. Who knows. Might even trigger a nuclear confrontation."

"Just the threat of such a thing would be a major terror weapon," Imelda said thoughtfully. Fortunately, Hadley had taken a seat back at the desk and Imelda was in frame.

"It would, wouldn't it?" Kellie asked, more to herself than the other two. She took a few minutes to wrap things up, obviously distracted.

"I didn't mean to terrorize you," Hadley said after helping Kellie get the camera and gear bags loaded into the van.

"It isn't that..." Kellie started to say, but suddenly realized she was actually terrified. "Well, I suppose it is. Partly. I had a theory... But what you and Imelda pointed out goes so much further."

"Well, look. I don't want to scare you. There are things you can do." Hadley looked around, lowered his voice, and then leaned forward slightly to say, "I'm a prepper, you see. I prepare for such things. Not just fungal plant diseases, but nuclear war, financial collapse, violent storms, all sorts of things. If you want some information, here is my card. Has my e-mail address on it. When the time comes, I think it would help make you feel better. Maybe even make doing your job easier if you are ready."

Kellie took the card and glanced at it. She looked up at Hadley. "Yes. Yes, I think I will." She held out her hand and Hadley shook it firmly.

CHAPTER THREE

"This is Kellie Manson reporting for Stringer News Network."

"The question of what will happen in St. Louis has been answered. But not the why or whom. A death toll of two hundred thousand and growing, from poisoned water sources, is the what. The Department of Homeland Security is working on the why and whom.

"Another news conference is scheduled for tomorrow in Memphis, Tennessee, due to the newest threat as seen on the internet. We will be there to cover what we all hope will be the announcement that DHS has caught the perpetrators and there will be no more incidents."

"You okay, Kellie?" Marcy asked when Justin signaled they were off the air.

"I didn't look okay on air?" a suddenly more alarmed Kellie asked.

"No. You looked very good. Just the right mix of professionalism and concern for people. I mean you. You just look... different."

Kellie forced a smile. She was tired. She hadn't slept much the night before, after talking to Hadley and Imelda. She had stashed the video, without telling anyone about the situation.

When she'd told Marcy that she didn't have anything they could use, Marcy had shrugged it off. "There is always a lot more video shot than is ever used. Still good that you are doing things on your own. Gives a lot more of an effect than just reading the news, even if that is all you do have to do. The trying and caring come through."

Then the call at four that morning, when the poisoning reports started coming in. They'd all been up since then. There wasn't a bottle of water to be found anywhere after eight o'clock in the morning. Kellie had made sure, as soon as they had word of what was going on; to get the crew to stock up before the inevitable happened.

Now on the way to Memphis, the crew all rather subdued from the savageness of the events they were covering, Kellie got online and sent Hadley an e-mail to make that second contact. Then she went exploring again. Looking for ways to become more prepared.

She quickly realized that she did lead a somewhat prepared lifestyle, always having some food and water in the apartment where she'd lived, and now in her jump bag, along with a change of clothes, some toiletries, make up, spare shoes, and cash.

Rather minor compared to what some people were doing, obviously, but she did already see the need and have the mindset to do more than what she was already doing.

Hadley responded to the e-mail much more quickly than Kellie expected and they soon went to a Skype connection to talk directly rather than pass e-mails back and forth.

"You're okay, aren't you?" Hadley asked her immediately. "Got safe water and all?"

"Yes. And you?" Kellie found she was a bit more concerned than she probably should be about Hadley.

"Oh, yes. I've plenty of stored water and the means to treat more. I saw you on TV. You handle yourself well on camera."

"Thanks Hadley," Kellie replied. She decided to get right down to business. "I've been doing some research on the internet about survivalists and preppers. I'd heard of survivalists, but not so much preppers. At least until that one TV show began to air. And they seemed the same. But I have a feeling you are more prepper than survivalist, according to some of my colleagues definitions."

"You are so right," Hadley said. Kellie could tell it was a heartfelt comment.

"I'd just as soon not get into a discussion of the difference, since you do understand already that there is a difference. I was a little worried about that."

"Because I'm a journalist?" Kellie asked.

"Mostly, yes. And you did mention you were from the east coast..."

"Ah. True. I can see where that might bother you, with the propensity of the majority to be more than a bit liberal in their thinking."

"Putting it mildly, but yes."

"Well, I've decided to jump onto this bandwagon with both feet, without waiting for the next event in Memphis."

"I heard that. You're already on the way?"

"Yes. But I want to get some preliminary ideas from you about getting ready for anything that might happen."

"Yes. Of course. Start with water. This was a good lesson on the importance of it."

"Okay..."

They talked for almost an hour about basic prepping. On how Kellie could be as safe as possible on the road as well as at home if the events became, as they feared, long term in effect. Just before they shut down Skype, Hadley gave her the web-site addresses of several forums where she could learn more, as well as a list of vendors she might want to use, soon, to get some supplies in the pipeline before things became too bad.

Kellie, between doing more basic research on al-Qaida and terrorism in general, for the next three days, had time to do a little specialty shopping on her own. She stashed the five small totes here and there in the vehicles, drawing the occasional comment. But all were joking and no one asked what she was shopping for.

Feeling a bit more prepared, Kellie hurried to the control truck when Marcy called her on the radio on the third day. Marcy was in the process of discussing what to do with home base, since nothing had been forthcoming in Memphis.

"Just got word to expect something today. Another internet warning. A bit less coherent than the others, but similar. Get Justin and yourself ready to go on at a moment's notice. We may have to do this one on the fly."

Kellie hurried out and found Justin to tell him what Marcy had said. As Justin equipped himself, Kellie hurriedly went to the bathroom, and then checked her appearance. She decided to change from the blouse and slacks she had on and pulled out one of the purchases she'd made that was in her locker on the bus, not in the totes.

Dressed in sturdy khaki pants, and a chambray shirt, with hiking boots on, Kellie scrubbed her face, applied just a touch of makeup, put on the new leather jacket, and then joined Justin. Her appearance brought a couple of glances, but no comments.

After double checking her jump bag and insisting Justin do the same, the two settled in to wait.

They didn't have to wait long. Kellie was squatting down, checking the jump bag one more time when the explosion came. It knocked her sideways and she got the first of many scuff marks on the leather jacket, turning it instantly into the 'weathered' class.

Justin was standing, talking to Marcy. The explosion threw Marcy into him and he went down hard, with her on top of him. There were people down all over. Only a half a dozen, sitting in the vehicles, weren't knocked down.

Hal, the medic for the group, since he was a trained paramedic, current with his licensing, as well as the chief soundman, began to quickly check on people.

Marcy climbed off Justin and helped him sit up. He groaned and turned white as a sheet for a moment. "I'm going to be sick."

Justin rolled to his side. But he dry heaved, without expectorating anything. After a few moments, with Kellie and Marcy both now kneeling beside him, he said, "Man that hurt! Cracked my left elbow. Thought I'd broken it."

Hal was there now and quickly checked Justin over. "Banged up, but okay. I'll give you something mild for the pain."

"You going to be able to handle the camera?" Marcy asked. Everyone was cross trained in several job positions, but Justin was undoubtedly the best camera person they had.

"Let me get that stuff from Hal," Justin said, getting to his feet slowly. "I'll be okay. But Kellie better drive."

"You sure, Justin?" Kellie asked. When he nodded and Hal hurried back over with a pill in a paper cup and a bottle of water, Kellie picked up the camera and ran over to the van she'd used before. There was no problem a few minutes later identifying where they needed to be. But there was a problem getting there.

Justin worked the GPS mapping system, looking for alternate routes to the site of the explosion, where a small mushroom cloud was beginning to dissipate. The thought of radiation had crossed both their minds, but the instruments in the vehicles were silent.

Kellie doubled back three times, but finally got to the edge of the devastated area. Justin had the camera ready and was out and ready when Kellie ran around the front of the van to take the microphone from him.

She surveyed the scene quickly, looked up at the sound of a helicopter. "Sure would be nice to be up there," she thought, and then pointed out a good shot, and waited for Justin's signal. The camera was on his shoulder and the light was on. The indicator went red and Justin made a motion with one hand. She was being recorded.

Barely two words into her intro, Justin mouthed the words, "We're live!"

Kellie blinked, but that was the only sign she gave that she was now on a live broadcast, the transmitter on Justin's back linking to the satellite truck, and it broadcasting to the SSN studios.

CHAPTER FOUR

"This is Kellie Manson reporting for Stringer News Network.

"There has been a tremendous explosion in the downtown area of Memphis. As you can see behind me, it was large enough to create a mushroom cloud, but there are no indications of radiation. I repeat there are no indications of radiation at this time.

"I'm not sure what could have caused an explosion this big, but it is without doubt the event threatened to occur here several days ago by terrorists."

Justin stepped to one side and Kellie smoothly transitioned to describing what he had the camera on. There were people frantically digging through the wreckage, looking for survivors.

"There!" she suddenly said loudly, pointing to a small group of people that were yelling and calling for help.

"It looks like they need help," Kellie said. "Someone smaller to..." She didn't really think about it, but tossed Justin the mike and took off running.

Justin, the pro that he was, kept the camera on Kellie, caught the mike, and began to follow her, despite the pain. It was against the unwritten rules of journalism of not getting involved, but Kellie joined right in the rescue operation, and Justin followed Kellie right up to the group.

She was already diving into the small opening in the side of a building from which screaming was coming. Everyone was covered with dust and mud, and there were already some flames from natural gas pipes that had been damaged.

Justin was aware peripherally of one of the helicopters coming down a lot closer to the ground.

People were frantic until first one young child, and then another came out of the hole. They were grabbed by two people each and hustled away, toward advancing sirens.

It was long moments before an elderly woman wiggled her way out of the hole and was helped to her feet. A dirty, wet Kellie came crawling out seconds before flame shot out of the hole, adding a bit more wear and tear to her jacket and pants.

This time the image that millions were seeing wavered somewhat as Justin followed Kellie at a run away from the building. But the SNN helicopter camerawoman had a steady cam shot of her and Justin.

Out of breath, Kellie finally stopped and Justin did as well. He spun around, barely in time to catch the explosion as more trapped gas from the broken natural gas lines exploded.

It was miniscule in relation to the earlier blast, but for those in the immediate area it was a warning to back off until more help could arrive and the gas lines could be isolated.

Kellie had the microphone in hand again and was describing the destruction. The rest of the crew had arrived and was now set up. Kellie waved Hal away when he approached to treat the obvious minor wounds.

She did stand still when he held up an earpiece a few moments later. He got her wired and stepped back. She was already listening to Marcy feed her information.

"Authorities are estimating that the initial explosion was caused by some ten thousand tons of... Ten thousand tons?

Yes, I am being told ten thousand tons of ANFO industrial explosives.

“This explosion dwarfed that of the nine hundred tons of LPG in Chicago. Death toll estimates are approaching hundreds of thousands more than Chicago.

“At this time, no one has stepped forward to claim responsibility for this terror attack, just as no one has the previous ones.

“This attack is in the WMD class. As destructive as a small nuclear weapon, except without the radiation. We will have further news as soon as it becomes available.”

Again Kellie held her stance until Justin let the camera sag. Then both sagged themselves. Hal was right there to check Kellie over while some of the others helped Justin with the camera and then to one of the vehicles where he could sit down.

“Ow!” Kellie exclaimed softly when Hal dabbed some medication on her cuts and abrasions.

“You’re lucky you had on the leather, from the looks of it,” Hal said, finally stepping back.

“You are some kind of a hero now,” Marcy said, coming over from the command truck to talk to Kellie. “I was ready to brain you when you took off like that, but the viewers are eating it up. Between Justin and the helicopter coverage, it was obvious you were right in the middle of a dangerous situation.”

“I didn’t do it for viewers,” Kellie said quietly. “People needed help that no one else could provide.”

"I know, Kellie. But don't denigrate yourself too much. That was a heroic thing to do. And since it was caught on video, you are going to have to cope with it. How you do will cement or destroy your reputation. Deny it being anything remarkable and people will feel you have no compassion. Talk it up too much, and they will decide you are just an airhead looking for fame."

"I guess you are right," Kellie said softly. "I just reacted. Not very good journalism, I know."

Marcy smiled. "Well, between the two, I'll take three live survivors and a hero over journalism any day."

Kellie finally smiled. "Yeah. I think I agree." Kellie's cell phone rang and she turned away to answer it as Marcy hurried back to the control truck.

"Are you all right? I saw you go into that building!" It was Hadley.

"I'm fine, Hadley! It wasn't that... Okay. It was scary. But no one else there could fit into the hole to get to the people. Some cuts and abrasions, but nothing serious. It was just something that needed to be done."

"Well... try not to do that kind of thing again. It scared me."

"Oh, Hadley! That is so sweet!"

"Uh... Yeah... I guess I have kind of fallen for you."

"Hadley, we barely know each other."

"I know. But... I guess I'd better let you get back to it. SNN said they were going back live after the commercial."

"Bye, Hadley," Kellie said quickly. "And... and I feel the same, Hadley."

Marcy was waving frantically at Kellie. Kellie ran over to the command truck.

"You're being interviewed, live, in a minute or so. Get ready."

"Interviewed?"

"Yes. Carla Jones."

"Carla?"

Marcy just looked at her. "I guess I'd better get a little more presentable..." Kellie said.

"Too late," called over Hal. "I need to wire you again."

Justin was already setting up another camera for the interview as Hall clipped the earpiece into place, and then the lapel microphone.

Marcy was standing beside Justin, counting down, a pair of headphones over her ears. The last finger went down and Marcy pointed at Kellie.

By the time the interview was over, Kellie was sure why SNN organizers had chosen Carla Jones as one of their key anchors. She got more out of Kellie than Kellie knew she had in her.

It was only by sheer will of effort that Kellie didn't blurt out her thoughts on the dangers to the food supply when asked her opinion of what the ultimate goal of the terrorists might be. It was more of a rhetorical question, anyway, but it hit close to home for Kellie.

"You did good, kid," Marcy said after the interview. "Now, we're going to wrap up here and head to New Orleans. You can go back to the hotel, clean up, and then catch up with us."

"New Orleans?" Kellie asked.

"Next target. Just got word," Marcy replied.

"Oh, no! Not another one?"

"Same group from what the internet is showing. Now get going. We've managed a real scoop here today. Let's be in a position to do it again, if we must, in New Orleans."

Kellie nodded. If it was to be, she wanted to be the one covering it. But what would it be this time?

She took the van back to the hotel, took a shower and changed into fresh clothing. She took time to get something to eat before heading out again, to pick up the SNN news convoy.

Kellie called after fueling the van to let them know she was on the way. The convoy would be travelling at the best speed for the slowest vehicles and she shouldn't have a problem catching up if she ran the speed limit.

She knew the address for the hotel where they would be staying, but caught up with the convoy just before they hit New Orleans proper and followed them into the parking lot.

She'd listened to the radio the whole trip and heard nothing new. Though she was sure Marcy would have contacted her if anything important had happened, the first thing Kellie did when everyone began to exit the vehicles and stretch was to find her and ask, just in case.

"No. The only thing we're getting is the internet broadcasts seem to be getting more aggressive and threatening. This last one promised an ultimatum of some kind."

"I need to take a look at that," Kellie said.

"Yes. Get your room assignment and see if you can make anything of it. I have a feeling we aren't going to have three days before whatever happens here, happens."

Kellie nodded and hurried off. She wanted to see that video.

It was different, just as Marcy had said. Though dressed the same, in black clothing and black ski mask, it was a different person reading the statement. Much more excitable. And also, as Marcy had said, at the end of the statement that New Orleans would feel Allah's wrath, the man calmed down slightly, looked at the camera and spoke without referring to a written statement.

Though she couldn't understand directly, the man's tone and the fire in his eyes were clear enough to make a shiver go down her back when the words were translated. "Make no mistake. These events have a purpose. That purpose will become clear very soon."

Not quite the ultimatum that Marcy indicated, but the words could easily be taken to mean that. Kellie sat back in the desk chair and began to think.

But it was time for supper and Marcy wanted to keep everyone close in case of a break in the story, so they were all eating in the same restaurant, though at several different tables, in small groups. Kellie joined Marcy and Justin at the table where they had taken seats.

"Just checking on Justin," Marcy said.

"How are you doing, Justin?" Kellie asked. "Maybe you should have stayed and seen a doctor and come down with me."

"Naw. Hal fixed me right up with a brace and some stuff to put on the elbow if it gets to hurting. I'm fine for the camera."

Marcy looked over at Kellie. "He sound okay to you?"

Justin frowned, but when Kellie gave him a long look, and then told Marcy, "I think so. He wouldn't jeopardize the operation."

"That was my thought, exactly. Now, what did you think of the internet broadcast."

"You were right. Different guy and different attitude. He was excitable. Until that last statement. I have a feeling things are going to get worse before they get better."

"Yeah. Those other guys were soldiers. This one is a fanatic, unless I miss my guess," Justin said.

The three paused to give their orders to the server that stopped at the table.

"Any speculation on the target here in New Orleans?" Kellie asked. SNN had some very good sources, though none had been on track of the earlier event. But things were marginally different now.

Marcy shook her head. "Odds are running from the Super Dome to the levees. Not sure what they could do to the levees, but it has been a different mechanism each time, though two were explosions. Each was a different type. DHS will be implementing aircraft restrictions in the area starting tomorrow morning."

Kellie's eyes widened. "They got that out of them? Can we use it?"

Marcy shook her head. "No. Not until the official announcement. But the risk of a plane being involved is now pretty slim. We'll key on something else. Unfortunately, they didn't tell me what, other than to forget about planes."

"Hm." Kellie looked thoughtful. Anything could be a target. With any type of attack. The three talked quietly of technical subjects while they waited for the food, and then ate heartily, the thought in the back of their minds that they might not have a chance to get breakfast.

But they were able to order it the next morning, just not finish it. They experienced yet another explosion, which rattled the windows in the restaurant where they had stopped to eat on the way to city hall for an announcement. The ground shook a few seconds later and the lights in the restaurant went out.

Again the direction was easy to spot. And like the ANFO explosion, there was a mushroom cloud. This one was much larger and as the convoy headed that direction at high speed, toward the Port of New Orleans, with the vehicles that would run most of them fortunately, several people began to monitor the radiation instruments some of the vehicles were equipped with. Sure enough, as they approached, the monitors began to sound a warning. There was radiation. A lot of radiation.

Marcy had been watching the weather and when she saw that they were driving right into the teeth of the wind coming from the mushroom cloud she ordered a quick right turn and ordered the convoy to go to high risk mode.

The drivers kept the vehicles close; everyone with any sort of camera that worked was getting what footage they could as the convoy cut across the path of the fallout that was now mostly a light rain. The radiation alarms began to go quiet and Marcy had the lead vehicle stop in the first open area where they could get a clear shot of the Port and the still rising mushroom cloud.

"Stay on those monitors!" Marcy directed several people. "Any sign of additional radiation and sing out!"

Hal was getting Kellie wired and Justin, along with assistant camera people, was setting up cameras and some monitoring instruments. Both for weather conditions and radiation.

"The wind changes and someone let me know," Marcy added to the instructions she was shouting out. She slipped the headphones over her head, talked to everyone now on the hot link, and told Kellie she was going live in just a few seconds.

As she usually did, Marcy fed Kellie information as she received it from various sources, local and distant. Kellie was adept at listening and then talking with barely a break in the rhythm of her broadcast.

CHAPTER FIVE

"This is Kellie Manson reporting for Stringer News Network.

"As you can see behind me, a nuclear device of some type has been detonated on the shoreline in the Port of New Orleans. There is radiation and some fallout. Our sources are telling us that there is an immediate evacuation order for the area and areas downwind of the blast.

"We went through a light rain of radiation but got through it. We are monitoring the winds and radiation live at the moment and may have to move if the radiation fallout swings this way.

"Our sources are saying this is approximately the same size detonation as the one in Memphis, only nuclear in type rather than ANFO, with attendant amounts of destruction. But the radiation is a factor this time and..."

Someone on the crew yelled as the winds changed suddenly. Justin had made sure that a radiation monitor was close and he cut to it as the person holding it held it up.

He cut back to Kellie. She started walking backwards, very slowly Justin thought, toward the command truck as he followed her with the camera, keeping the shot going.

"We will set up again as soon as we find a safe place. This is Kellie Manson reporting for SNN. Please follow all instructions you receive from the authorities. This is not a movie or a trick. This is a real nuclear explosion. We'll be back with more live shots soon."

"Let's boogie, people!" Marcy yelled. She was plotting a course with the lead driver, on a GPS with a weather map overlay. "I'm riding up here," she told Kellie and Justin. You two stay with the command truck."

There was more jostling as people moved equipment from a couple more of the vehicles that would not now start to those that were still running, and joined their co-workers in the tight quarters.

Kellie helped to brace Justin as he continued to use the camera to get what shots he could as the convoy wove around dead vehicles and people running in the streets, going mostly the same way they were.

Twice they tried to stop and set up again, but New Orleans police waved them onward frantically. But Marcy and the lead driver were good. Another fifteen minutes and they were able to set up again. Three minutes later Kellie was back on the air.

"This is Kellie Manson reporting for Stringer News Network. We are again out of the path of the fallout and live on scene of the New Orleans nuclear attack. We have managed to get additional information from official sources.

"The device seems to have been meant primarily to disrupt the oil flow from off-shore rigs and tanker deliveries here in the port, as it did, in fact knock out those facilities where they come from the Port waters onto land. No estimates as to when production might start again.

"Death toll estimates..." Kellie gasped, but immediately continued. "Three hundred thousand, with additional projected loss of life as high as one million..."

Kellie dodged when a New Orleans police officer tried to grab the hand mike from her. She saw Justin go down under an onslaught of three officers, the camera lens still on her until the very last.

No one had seen the group of officers approach. Only when the attack was in full swing on Justin and Kellie did the others start to fight back.

Justin was up as quickly as possible and got a very good zoom shot of Kellie being hit in the face by the gloved fist of one of the officers. She staggered, but didn't go down. She jerked the microphone free of another's grasp and brought it up to her bloody lips.

Half a dozen shots were fired, though no one was hit, before Marcy called her people off and agreed to vacate the area peacefully. Though the officers were shouting to turn off all cameras, people were using camera phones and everything else to record the altercation.

Kellie had taken the brunt of the attack, after Justin, as the other officers mostly just kept the rest of the news team at bay. They had seemed intent on preventing any coverage of the disaster.

Hal was in the command truck with Kellie and Justin, tending to Kellie's injuries. Justin had fared fairly well, protecting both the camera and his left arm when he'd been taken down.

It was another twenty minutes before Marcy stopped the convoy. They were at a check point, staffed with National Guard personnel. The various media people had an area set aside for them and a Public Information Officer told them that there would be a news conference in just a few minutes.

Well practiced now, though with only half their equipment working, Marcy had the team set up and ready well before the PIO called for attention.

Kellie had waved off make up; preferring to go on camera without any concealing effects hiding the damage the police had done to her face.

She got through the nearly useless information release without a bobble, but had to wipe angry tears away when she thrust the microphone toward the PIO and asked why New Orleans Police were attacking media personnel. Justin had the camera on the PIO immediately after the shot of Kellie wiping her eyes.

"We have no evidence of such happenings," replied the PIO. Justin just managed to catch the incredulous look on Kellie's face when he cut back to her.

Marcy told Kellie they were getting instructions from home base and to cut it short. Kellie did so, obviously angry. She signed off and she and Justin joined Marcy as the others began to break down the equipment at Marcy's quick indication to do so.

"Okay," Marcy said, taking the head set off and setting it aside. "We're lodging a formal complaint, and asking for criminal charges."

Kellie managed to smile and relax slightly.

"You are so going to have a shiner," Marcy said, taking a closer look at Kellie's left eye.

"Yeah. Whatever," Kellie said, no longer concerned with the event. SNN was dealing with it. There wasn't much she could do but wear the signs for as long as they existed. "Anything further on the nuke attack? An announcement yet?"

Marcy shook her head. "And I guess we just have to wait. Going to try and get the rest of our equipment recovered and ready to go. Do some more coverage of the cleanup and wait for something else from the terrorists. Home base is sending down another crew. With Carla. She'll be taking over this coverage tomorrow."

Marcy watched Kellie carefully. She'd been asked to, specifically, but would have anyway. Kellie surprised her just slightly. But on retrospect, not that much.

"Okay. Good. She knows this stuff better than I do and can probably get some government officials to talk. I'm not in a position to do that yet.

"And I'd rather be free to cover more of the story. I don't think this is anywhere near the end."

"You think more than just a statement about what the terrorist want?" Justin asked. "That was my feeling from that last terrorist video."

"I don't know. Just a gut feeling," Kellie said. "That could be the beginning of another stage. Like Marcy said, no way of knowing until they decide to do something else."

"Kellie is right. And for right now, I want to do a piece on our equipment. There was an EMP, obviously, but only some of the equipment went down and other items continued to work, fortunately for us. I think we had the highest rate of working equipment. Home base instructed me to make our broadcast equipment available to the other services that need it."

"Aw, man!" Justin said. "With that kind of exclusive?"

"They want good relations with the other networks. We could be in the same position at some point." Marcy smiled then.

"And with the number and kind of scoops I think we may be doing, we're going to need some good will up front."

"Good point," Justin said. "Okay. I'm going to secure what I've got and then we can start on the equipment report. That okay, Kellie?"

"You might want to go and get cleaned up some," Marcy said.

Kellie shook her head. "Let's get it while it is fresh. I'm curious, anyway. I didn't really think anything would work after a nuke."

"Do it up good and we'll see if we can finagle a feature piece out of it."

Marcy moved off and Justin and Kellie headed for one of the trucks that had secure media storage to put away what he had and get fresh media and batteries.

"Something of a come down, all of a sudden," Justin said a few minutes later, after talking to Hal about the EMP and waiting on another of the electrical crew for her opinions.

Kellie shook her head. "There's always something to do. This could be important information at some point, for someone. I have a couple of sources online that I'll check tonight and find out what I can. If I can."

"Okay. I'm happy if you're happy."

They were interrupted once, for Kellie to calm down Hadley. He'd been watching the coverage and had seen Kellie attacked by the police. He'd only just been able to get the cell phone coverage through.

"I'm still working, Hadley. But I'm okay. Home base is taking steps, which is confidential, by the way. Working on an EMP story. Anyone you can recommend I talk to?"

Hadley gave Kellie a couple of names and website addresses and reluctantly let her go back to work.

"You and this Hadley?" Justin asked, with a grin.

"Yeah. I don't know. Maybe. He's a good guy. I like him. You would, too."

It was a tired crew that finally called it a night and found another hotel that could take them all. They had to do some doubling up, but everyone had their own bed, and most of the equipment was back online, with a lot of money spent to get it so.

Kellie did a short piece with Carla again, the next day, about the police attack on the news crew. Kellie hadn't really had a chance to see the footage Justin had captured and was amazed at how intense and firm she'd been during the event. She'd been angry, and more than a little scared. The anger had showed, but the scared hadn't.

With Carla there doing the brunt of the work of covering the nuclear attack, Marcy and her crew was ordered to take a break, see to getting the rest of the equipment repaired or replaced, and to work on the production of the EMP piece, which home base had decided to run with.

Kellie convinced Marcy that Hadley was a good information resource for the EMP and related subjects and talked her into taking the crew back to St. Louis to talk to him, and several people he managed to talk into talking to Kellie.

They took their time, to give time for Hadley to get some things set up and just in case something broke on the terror story. There had been no new videos, not even a follow up on the stated news to come.

Most of the crew was at the hotel in St. Louis, taking it easy, with Kellie, Justin, Hal, Marcy, and a couple of other techs at Hadley's home for an interview.

The college had denied permission for them to do anything at the school, and a couple of the people that Hadley had arranged for had refused to be anywhere public.

Justin and Hal were really getting into the subject of EMP and seemed intrigued that the two men that were supposedly experts on the subject chose to appear only in silhouette and have their voices altered or they wouldn't talk.

It amused Marcy more than a little. She decided they just wouldn't use any of the nonsense. She'd been a better than fair editor at one time in her career and would be in on the edit for this piece to make sure it came across professional.

She changed her mind a little when the two men, between them, produced several government documents about EMP that were not in public circulation.

It was the second day of the interview, with Hadley and the other two watching the footage that Justin and Kellie had done on their own equipment after the EMP had zapped them in New Orleans, before they gave their opinions on the whys and wherefores of what had happened.

Much to everyone's annoyance, Marcy's cell phone rang. But when she quickly hung up and asked Hadley if he had an internet connection, the annoyance vanished. "The ultimatum is out," Marcy said.

With everyone gathered around, Hadley got on the internet, switched the feed to the large screen TV in his den, and found the video.

All of them watched silently until it was over.

The United States would begin to fulfill a thirty step process or 'Allah's Warriors' would institute, in addition to more, similar attacks, a program to infect major basic food crops with fungal diseases. Not only in the US, but in all countries that continued to support the Great Satan.

Kellie looked over at Hadley in alarm. "You were so right," she said softly.

Marcy's cell phone rang again. "Yes. We're on it."

She closed the phone and addressed the small group. "We have to head back to New Orleans. Carla is going back to New York to cover this new threat. Where are we going to find anyone on short notice that is an expert on fungal plant diseases? We have to find out just what this means."

Softly, Kellie said, "We have a major scoop, Marcy. Hadley is our expert. I've already got a lot of preliminary footage on just this possibility."

"What? What are you talking about? That theory you had before?" Marcy asked. She studied Kellie closely, but that confident look was there, as always.

"Give me a minute," Kellie said and ran out of the house. She was back in less than a minute with a thumb drive in her hand. She handed it to Hadley. "Play that."

Kellie looked over at Marcy. "See what you think."

They were barely ten minutes into the recordings when Marcy was calling out on her cell phone. She moved away and talked quietly for a good three minutes as the others continued to watch the video.

“Hadley,” Marcy said when she put the phone away, can I use your internet connection for a bit?”

“Sure,” Hadley said. “What do you want me to do?”

“Just make sure I have a good connection.” She looked over at Sally, one of the techs. “Get my computer case.”

“You’re welcome to use my computer,” Hadley said.

Marcy grinned. “Mine’s encrypted for secure comms with home base. I want them to see this.” She nodded toward the TV screen.

“Sorry guys,” Marcy said a couple of minutes later when everyone gathered around her at the desk. “This is top secret. I need to do this in private.”

Reluctantly, the others left, Hadley removing the thumb drive from his computer and handing it to Marcy.

The two men, after asking if they were needed any longer and when told no, left. Kellie and the others heard one tell the other, “I’m calling Emergency Essentials and Canning Pantry as soon as I get home.”

The other had responded, “Yeah. Me, too. And Rainy Day Foods. Maybe Nitro-Pak.”

Justin and Hal looked at Kellie and Hadley. Sally and June were over in a corner, discussing something.

Hadley realized they were wondering what the two men were talking about. "Long term food storage foods," Hadley said. "Emergency Essentials, Rainy Day Foods, and Nitro-Pak sell foods suitable for long term storage. Canning pantry sells jars and canners to put up food by home canning, along with a lot of other products."

"That kind of sounds like it might be a good idea," Justin said. He looked at Hal.

"Yeah," Hal said. "Depends on how this plays out, but yeah. Wish I knew a little more about this. Gonna have to do some quick research."

"Uh..." Hadley hesitated for a minute, but finally said, "I guess I can give you some information... Show you some of what I have." He made a point not to look at Kellie. Sally and June moved over to join the group.

Kellie decided she might as well admit that she was in prepper mode herself. "He knows what he's talking about. I've already made some purchases from those companies," Kellie told her friends and co-workers.

"You're a survivalist?" asked June.

Kellie shook her head. "Prepper. Just beginning. Hadley, you explain."

Hadley dropped into lecture mode and began to show the group some of what he was prepping. It was the first time that Kellie realized just how much of a prepper he actually was.

Marcy had to come looking for them, in the basement.

"Hey! It's a go. Hadley, you are ours, exclusively, for a while, right?"

With Kellie looking at him expectantly, Hadley quickly nodded. "Whatever I can do. Exclusively to SNN and Kellie."

Kellie started, and so did Marcy. The other four exchanged a glance.

After a moment Marcy nodded. "Doable."

"But Carla," Kellie protested.

"She won't stand in the way. I'm sure of it. You've got the scoop. You deserve to run with it. Now, let's get back to the hotel and get things set up. We go live in ninety minutes."

CHAPTER SIX

"This is Kellie Manson reporting for Stringer News Network.

"Joining me today is Hadley Robertson. Renowned authority on fungal diseases of food plants.

"After a video presentation, he will be answering further questions on the fungal diseases and explaining what this new terror threat could mean.

"And now that video."

They were not only first, but pretty much the only, authority on the subject. Of course others looked for their own experts, and found them, but none to match Hadley's knowledge, passion on the subject, and already well thought out insights of what the wide spread fungal infection of the US food supply would mean.

Despite Hadley's assurances that SNN and Kellie would have the exclusive, when he was contacted by DHS and ordered to Washington for consultation with the authorities, he really couldn't say no. He would be going to Washington voluntarily, or in handcuffs as a potential terrorist himself.

Carla would be handling the lead on the threat, but Kellie, without much problem, convinced Marcy that since she was probably out of that loop now, that they cover what people were going to do to prepare for the event.

There wasn't a single person that would come out and say that the US would do any of the thirty steps required for the terrorists to back down, much less all of them.

It was up to DHS to prevent the event, if possible, and for everyone else to prepare for it the best they could. They had until planting time that spring in the southern states, which was the deadline Allah's Warriors had given to implement the plan.

With Hadley finally loose from DHS clutches, having given them all the expertise they could use, he again became Kellie's primary advisor on Prepping, personally, and getting the message across to the public.

Kellie was left with a small team to do the series of reports and Marcy took the rest of the crew on to California to cover the story from the west coast with another on-air reporter, with Carla lead in New York.

Kellie had the responsibility to produce a twenty minute segment for airing in a half hour time slot every Sunday until something was resolved.

Her team was into the project solidly. It was the same group that had been at Hadley's when the ultimatum was broadcast, minus Marcy. Kellie acted as producer and on-air reporter, with Sally assistant producer, June the general purpose member including gopher, with Justin and Hal the production team.

All of them got into prepping in a big way, learning as they went and making group purchases of items to reduce costs. Hadley didn't say so specifically, but he essentially opened up his small estate to them as not only their headquarters, but as a shelter of last resort if things got as bad as they possibly could.

Kellie he told right out that she had a place here with him if she ever needed it in the future. Kellie acknowledged the remark, but had decided, for the meantime, to keep it strictly professional with Hadley. It was a difficult task at times, as she learned more and more about him during their work time together.

There had been no more overt attacks, despite the warning from Allah's Warriors. Some possible ones Kellie had covered in the series.

The series began to get good reviews and solid viewership, bringing prepping into the mainstream, without the hype and theatrics of some earlier shows. Kellie was presenting good, solid, well researched information to the public on how to deal with not only the possibility of food shortages in the future, but with natural disasters of all types.

But suddenly DHS was back at Hadley's place, this time with a message for Kellie. Cease and desist the series, or else. "Your superiors are being given the same message, but it would behoove you to take this as a personal request from some powerful people, no matter what SNN might say or do."

The woman, who could have been in a "Men In Black" movie from the way she was dressed, had taken no more than a minute and a half to flash her credentials, give Kellie the message, and then leave.

Kellie was immediately on the phone with SNN. She was shocked to learn that she no longer had any ties with SNN and would be receiving a severance package within a week.

When she looked around she saw that Hal, Justin, Sally, and June were all on their cell phones. Kellie had heard them all ring while she was getting the bad news.

She saw each of the four try to protest something, but then each slowly put away their cell phone and looked over at Kellie.

"Kellie..." Justin paused for a moment, but took a deep breath and continued. "I just got word I'm to head back to New York with all the equipment."

He looked around in surprise when Hal said almost the same thing. Hal, Justin, and Kellie looked at Sally and June. Both were nodding, and Sally said, "Same thing."

"And I've been let go," Kellie said, fighting back tears.

"What is going on?" Hadley asked, coming into the living room where everything was set up for the research.

"SNN just fired me," Kellie said. "DHS just told me to drop the project and that they were telling SNN the same thing. I didn't even have a chance to ask any questions."

"They fired you?" Justin asked. "But the series is going so good! And they're sending us to New York. Are you sure you didn't misunderstand?" he added hopefully.

Kellie shook her head. "No misunderstanding."

"Well... Look..." Hal looked at the other three and then back at Kellie. "Maybe we can keep working on it on the sly. You know. And sell it to another network."

Justin looked ready to agree, but Sally and June looked scared.

"I was told to come back immediately and break all ties with you, Kellie. That DHS had you under investigation."

"What?" Kellie asked. She looked at Justin, Hal, and June.

"Same thing with me," June said.

"No. No. That is not right!" Justin said angrily. "They just told me to come back with the equipment. Hal?"

"Nothing like that to me, either. But they did imply hanging around Kellie might not be a good idea. Not even to finish up anything we may have started for the next segment."

"I'm not going to take this sitting down," Justin said firmly. He looked at Kellie and started to reassure her that they would get to the bottom of it and find out what was going on.

But Kellie was shaking her head. "No. You can't Justin. Not any of you. They've singled me out. But you guys have a chance to keep going and getting better prepared. You all have lives that you need to protect. I'll deal with this on my own."

"No. You won't," Hadley said firmly and took her right hand into both of his hands. "This has turned tin-foil hat. Suddenly the government doesn't want the kind of knowledge you've been providing made public. Probably understand that you are getting close to some things that they really don't want known."

"Hadley, we haven't broadcast anything anti-government!" Kellie protested.

"Yet," Hadley replied. "I've seen you going over some of the more out there information. That brain of yours is making connections. Connections that DHS and the powers that be don't want made, much less broadcast by a popular journalist."

"The internment camps?" Justin asked softly.

Kellie sighed. “Among some others. I haven’t brought them up. I don’t know how I was going to handle them, or even if I was.”

“Internment camps?” asked June.

“Better you don’t ask,” Hadley said. “Sounds like you guys are getting a bye. I wouldn’t chance getting any more exposed on their radar.”

“I don’t like it,” Justin said. He was as stubborn as they come.

“I don’t either,” Hal said. “But I have Suzzie and the kids to worry about.” He gave Kellie a long look. “I’m sorry, Kellie.”

“It’s all right, Hal. I know you’ve been missing them. Only seen them a few times these last weeks.”

Justin glanced over at Sally and June and decided anything else he had to say he would say when they weren’t within earshot. “Okay. I guess we’d better break things down and get packed,” he said.

“I’ll help...”

“Best you don’t,” Hal said. “You don’t want to be in a position to be accused of trying anything with the equipment or data. Better to let us do it while you and Hadley decide how you’re going to handle things.”

“He’s right, Kellie,” Hadley said. He let her hand slide from his. “Come on. Let’s get a cup of tea and talk about this a bit.”

Kellie nodded, sadly, but followed Hadley to the kitchen. She waited, thinking, ignoring the murmurs and other sounds coming from the living room as the gear was packed up.

No sooner was the tea ready and the gear stacked by the front door of the house when a knock came. Hadley went to answer the door. There were three men there, and a van was driving away.

“We’re here to take the SNN employees and their equipment to St. Louis, and then to New York. This the gear?”

“Hey, now,” Justin said. “We have vehicles here and are quite capable of…”

“Not my department, chum,” said the obvious leader of the three.
“We’re here to load and drive. And we will be taking the company vehicles. All of them. Now let’s move. Our orders said this was high priority.”

Sally and June hurried to the door and outside. Hal hesitated, but then waved a small wave at Kellie, without going over or saying anything.

But as soon as the three men had picked up the first load of equipment and followed Hal and the two women out of the house, Justin ran over to Kellie and handed her one of his business cards. “Got another number on the back. Keep in touch.”

Justin looked at Hadley. “Learned a lot from you, man. Thanks. Take good care of her.” With that he spun on his heel and was back at the door, picking up his computer case when the three men came back inside for the second load.

“I’ll carry this one. My personal computer,” Justin said.

The leader of the three men didn’t like it much, but didn’t make an issue of it. He did wait for the other two men to take a second load of equipment out to the vehicles while he watched Hadley and Kellie, obviously guarding the equipment from their access.

When the two were back, all three loaded up with the last of the equipment and headed out, leaving the door open. Hadley, stiff as a board, walked over to the open door with Kellie and watched the three men get into the driver's seats of the three vans and then drive away.

It hadn't set well with him to have people in his home he hadn't invited. People that gave orders they had no right to give.

"You know," Kellie said, closing the door, "I don't think those are SNN drivers. You think Justin and the others will be all right?"

Hadley thought for a moment, but nodded. "Yeah. I think so. If they were going to really strong arm them, I don't think they would have been called first to get ready."

Kellie leaned against Hadley suddenly and started to cry. But before Hadley could get her over to the sofa and get her sitting down she straightened back up and stepped back. She wiped her eyes angrily. "You remember when you said, 'When the time comes?'"

Hadley nodded.

"I am not going to let this go, Hadley. I might not be able to do much about what is going on now, but it isn't going to be a personal disaster for me. I won't let it."

She bit her lip, but continued. "But I need a place to stay for a while until..."

"You have one, Kellie. For as long as you want, under any circumstances you are comfortable with. And starting tomorrow, I'm going to bring you up to speed on all my preps."

Kellie managed to smile. "You've been holding out on me?"

Hadley smiled back. "Not you. The others, yeah, I guess so. But I couldn't put you in the position of needing to keep things from your friends, so I left a few things out when we were going over my preps."

"I guess the first thing I need to do is get my things from Los Angeles," Kellie said, moving away from Hadley, going back into the kitchen to get her tea, looking thoughtful.

"I just had most of what I ordered delivered to the same climate controlled storage facility I rented when SNN said they were moving me there. I wonder if they'll try to take back the signing bonus?"

Hadley could see that the tears were near, but Kellie blinked them away, lost in thought again. "I'm not going to be able to afford much more, so I'm going to need your help deciding what is critical." She looked over at Hadley, to see him watching her, sipping his own tea.

"Expenses don't have to be a problem," he said.

"No. I mean, yes, they do," Kellie said firmly. "I won't let you support me. I've done well for myself, and have more savings than you might imagine. And the SNN pay was very good, while it lasted. I was on the road most of that time and spent very little of it until I started buying preps. So, I'm okay. I don't want you to worry about me financially."

"Okay," Hadley said simply. He'd bring up the subject of taking care of her for the rest of their lives some other time. "When the time comes, though," he thought, "she won't talk me out of it."

CHAPTER SEVEN

Hadley joined Kellie at the table still set up in the living room. She had her personal lap top open and connected to the internet in the matter of a few moments.

"I think I'd better download everything I want from my files on the SNN servers I uploaded from my company computer before they think to cut me off. I'm sure they will. It is only good business sense. But I worked hard for some of that information and I plan on having it. Fortunately I'd backed up this morning so I'm not losing anything on the work computer they took."

Hadley stayed quiet while she worked on the computer. But when she was obviously finished with the task, he spoke, "Speaking of security, I think it might be a good idea to invoke a little ourselves and get out of town for a while."

Kellie looked startled for a moment, and then a bit cautious. "The money, Hadley. I don't want to spend a lot of money on motels and such. And I'm not ready to share a room with you."

"Nothing like that," Hadley quickly said. "It is also part of showing you more of my preps. This isn't the only property I own. I have a place in the Black Hills, in Wyoming. There would be a couple or three nights in motels, but that's all. Separate rooms, of course. On me if you'll let me."

"Oh. I... uh... don't know what to say. Except, no on letting you pay for my rooms. I can manage that. I just thought you meant going on the run and... I don't know. It just didn't occur to me you might have another place."

"Places," Hadley said with a broad smile. "Only one other similar to this one, but four of what I call minimal bug out locations. There is one near here, one near the place in the Black Hills, and two others in other parts of the country."

"Landed gentry?" Kellie was smiling, too.

"Something like that, yes. I seldom put all my eggs in one basket."

"Yeah. I'm learning just how much more true that is than I did at first. There is nothing really preventing me from going. I'm going to assume that the severance package they referred to will be sent to my mail drop, like the other things they have had to mail to me."

"Mail drop, huh? You do have a few surprises of your own."

It was Kellie's turn to grin widely. "Yes. I do, as a matter of fact. But if we're going to go, let's do it. You've already got me a little spooked."

Hadley nodded and stood up. "If you'll lend a hand shutting down the place, we can be on our way to pick up your things at the hotel, and then hit the road, in just a few minutes."

"You always ready to leave on a moment's notice?" Kellie asked.

"Pretty much," Hadley said, nodding. "I'll call in to the school and activate a more or less standing leave of absence. I've done it a couple of times before. They don't like it much, but they want me bad enough to agree to it."

It took all of ten minutes for Hadley to make the call, secure the place, including closing the security shutter system that protected all the windows and doors of the house.

Kellie was waiting for him outside, with her go bag and computer case when he drove out of the garage and triggered the garage door and shutter to close.

But he wasn't in the beat up old Subaru she'd seen him drive before. This time he was in a just as beat up old Chevy Suburban. There was a roof rack, covered with a tarp, a rear rack, also covered with a tarp, and a front rack. It too had a tarp covering whatever it was the rack carried. Only a large number of lights weren't covered, and there were some facing forward that were.

A winch was the only thing Kellie could think of that might be on the front bumper, but hurried over to get into the front passenger seat of the vehicle after putting the bags on the passenger side rear seat, without doing the exploring she would like to do. Hadley had mentioned a BOV, or bug out vehicle, as well as a PAWV, or post-apocalyptic world vehicle. Kellie had a feeling this was probably a PAWV.

Hadley pulled over to the detached garage, triggered a remote to open the security shutters and the garage door of one of the four bays. It was the matter of a few minutes for him to hook up to a large tandem wheel box trailer, just as beat up looking as the Suburban. It, too, had a tarped load on a roof rack and one on the tongue.

When the trailer was connected, Hadley triggered the remote again to close up the detached garage. Kellie watched the lights on the trailer when Hadley tested them. The two got back into the Suburban.

Kellie was surprised at the difference between the inside and outside of the vehicle. The outside had nicks and dents, not a spark of chrome, and a more or less tan and gray, not quite camouflage paint scheme, with a few primer covered points of sheet metal work, and the dirty work tarps.

The inside, on the other hand, sported pristine tan leather seats, four of them, and what wasn't behind some type of equipment, was upholstered with button tufted light brown leather. Sides and overhead both. And the floor was some sort of rugged rubber, also a light brown.

The dash, all of it, from left to right, had something neatly inserted, mostly electronics. They were barely visible through a series of tight copper mesh panels. There was an overhead platform, also loaded with gear, and a console from between the front seats up to the middle of the dash. All of them had the same copper mesh panels.

Hadley reached up to the overhead, lifted mesh panel and pressed two switches. Kellie heard a slight whine and then two faint thumps. "Erecting two of the taller roof rack mount antennas," Hadley told Kellie.

"Oh. I've never seen this much communications gear, except in the command and satellite trucks!"

"I like to keep informed," Hadley said, "and stay in touch. If you are ready, we'll be off."

"I guess so," Kellie replied. When Hadley put the Suburban in gear again, Kellie listened intently. "I know it is diesel, but I can barely hear it."

"Great exhaust system, and the engine compartment is well insulated for sound, temperature, as well as somewhat armored."

"Armored?" Kellie asked.

Hadley nodded. "Not substantially, but enough to get through some light rifle fire. Radiator is protected very well, and if I think there will be a likelihood to be attacked, I have some armor for the tires made of curtains of hard chain installed that I can deploy.

“The body has Kevlar armor covering the outside of the original sheet metal, and that is covered with the exterior sheet metal, over a full roll cage. Not too noticeable, but if you look close you can see that the overall dimensions are a bit larger all around than normal.

“But that thickness also helps conceal the fact that the windows are all two inch thick armor laminate, including the windshield. The front door windows open, but they swing out and up with pressure cylinder assistance, rather than roll down into the doors. Underneath the body has armor in strategic spots, too.

“We’re good up to .308 FMJ. That starts getting through. And I have wearable body armor packed in the back that will add additional protection, if we think we could be going into harms’ way.”

“Holy cow! I didn’t even know you could do that.”

“Not inexpensive, and I pay a weight penalty, but we’re as protected as we can be for a moderate investment. We can only do about a hundred ten, rather than the hundred thirty I was shooting for, and it takes some time to get to that speed, but I thought some armor was better than only speed and maneuverability.”

“I feel safer than I believe I ever have in a vehicle,” Kellie said.

“We’re vulnerable to mines and IEDs, but I consider them low probability and just didn’t want to go to a full armored vehicle.”

"Oh. Well, still safer than anything else I've ever been in. Hundred and ten, huh? Don't feel compelled to prove it."

Hadley laughed as Kellie snugged up the safety harness a little. He turned on the satellite radio when both fell silent, to listen to the news. In the time it took to get to the hotel in St. Louis they had not heard of anything of import.

But Kellie became livid again, keeping it well under control, when she found her key card wouldn't work on the hotel room door. They went down to the front desk and asked what the problem was.

The clerk was apologetic, and said, "I'm sorry. Your company called and said to close the account and evict you. That you would have to pay on your own."

"My things?" Kellie asked, quietly and calmly.

"I'll have the bell captain get them," said the clerk. "I assure you that your things were handled with the utmost respect and packed securely in your bags before they were moved."

"Yes. Of course. My *former* employer always went for quality. If you will hurry, I'd like to be on my way."

"You're not taking another room? I assure you that..."

"I think not," Kellie said.

Hadley had kept silent, watching Kellie work through her anger at the treatment. But she held tough and didn't take it out on the hotel staff, even giving the bell captain a modest tip for bringing out the bags on a cart to the Suburban.

"I'll handle the bags," Hadley told the man. He opened the split rear rack and then the Dutch door rear of the Suburban and Kellie took a good look at the construction. She could see that the total thickness of the exterior of the truck was much greater than normal.

She also got a good look at the built in boxes that lined the sides of the cargo compartment, leaving the center of the area open from the rear doors to the rear seats. There was plenty of space left after Hadley stacked her bags securely beside his.

After a stop for a fast food lunch, Hadley headed the Suburban west on I-44. Again they listened to the satellite radio as Hadley maneuvered among the heavy traffic, until well away from St. Louis. It was a normal news day and Hadley soon switched to a music station, and turned the volume down.

"Want to have something live going, in case something happens," Hadley told Kellie. "This station has news breaks as well as the music. But we can talk. I suppose I should tell you where we are going."

Kellie looked up from her intense study of the cockpit of the Suburban, trying to figure out just what everything was. "Yeah. I've been distracted, I guess. I should know something about where we're going."

"After we get your things in Los Angeles, we'll head for Hulett, Wyoming. Outside, actually. My family is from there, originally. Some of the early settlers. I own a hunting lodge up in the Black Hills that I inherited when my parents died. It is run by a small staff, and has two guides under contract to take people on hunting trips."

"I never really pictured you as a hunter," Kellie said.

"I don't, much. Not anymore. I did my share when I was growing up. But once I got into college and then began my career, I just never seem to have the time. Not even here in Missouri. My trips out to Robertson Lodge have all been working trips to supervise getting the place set up as more than a hunting lodge."

"Prepping stuff? A retreat or bug out location?"

"In a sense, it is a bug out location, though that isn't the primary function. It, like my place here, is a primary home with some aspects of an off grid homestead or estate. Places where I can live the majority of the time. The actual bug out locations aren't anywhere like the two major places."

Kellie nodded. "I think I understand. If you're living there, it isn't a bug out location. It is a home. You just happen to have two."

"Exactly. They are the bug in locations. And the minimal places are the bug out locations."

"You've done well for yourself," Kellie said.

"I inherited much of it, I have to admit," Hadley replied with a slight shrug. The hunting lodge property and business, which does moderately well. And I do well as a professor at the college, and have a few patents for disease control products for commercial crops that bring in extra money.

"I have some investments. Conventional as well as prep related. Rental income property including quadraplex housing units and investment in two farms, some specific stocks and mutual funds; I regularly buy and sell stock warrants, have some monetary investments in Switzerland, hold precious metals, set up two deferred annuities I'm paying into; and have a trust I'm also adding to. I'm a believer in diversification."

"I'll say!" Kellie laughed.

Hadley smiled over at her and added, "Plus I'm published. Two text books and quite a few magazine articles in my field. A couple of science tomes, again in my field. And there is more than enough income from the place here in Missouri to keep it going on its own. I'm doing okay."

"I didn't see anything that would make money at the place outside St. Louis!"

Hadley looked over and smiled. "I have experimental specialty crops I develop, for seed, for a couple of the major seed companies. Plus there is the really good fruit and nut orchard, vineyard, asparagus and berry patches that produce things for a farmers' market. You've seen those."

"Yes. I just didn't think about them as income."

"Enough to help pay the bills."

"Just how old are you?" Kellie suddenly asked, a worrisome thought entering her mind.

"Think I might be too old for you? I'm thirty. Just turned. I got an early start with the inheritance and have worked in some form or another since I was fifteen."

"I didn't mean to sound..." Kellie said softly. "I thought you were about my age... older, yes... but what you have people in their fifties often don't have. Thirty. That's good."

Hadley decided the best thing to do was leave the subject alone. If he was going to win Kellie's heart, as well as her mind, it was going to take some time. She had a shell he could tell, anyway, and the events of the day had suddenly made it much tougher and thicker.

They fell silent, enjoying the scenery and music. Hadley had already said they weren't going to push for minimum time, but take their time on the trip. Not a lot of sightseeing, but no five in the morning to nine at night constant runs.

It was after three when Hadley woke Kellie. She'd fallen asleep nearly an hour before. "Kellie. Kellie," he said softly.

It took Kellie a few moments to get oriented. But she looked over at Hadley.

"Don't really need fuel. I have plenty on board, but I like to keep the tanks topped off. And I need a bathroom break. Plus I want to decide where to stop for the night before we take off again."

Kellie yawned, but nodded.

They were stopped for less than fifteen minutes, most of that spent using the laptop in the Suburban, with a satellite internet link, to find and book rooms for the night for about six in the evening.

"I wish I had my camping gear. We could stay out a couple of nights on the way. On the way from LA to Hulett perhaps we can do that."

"I have all we need," Hadley said. "Even extra sleeping bags, and two tents, plus emergency shelters. But it is going to be really cold once we get a bit north. We can, if you want, or stop a couple of times on this leg. That'll be up to you."

"Hmm. Let me think about it. I'd really like to, but you have some good points. And I always preferred to camp out for several days, rather than just one night and move on."

"I'm the same way," Hadley said. "If I'm going to be out in the wilderness, I want to be there for a while. Day trips, sure, but setting up and breaking camp on a trip, unless that is the purpose of the trip, doesn't really interest me."

What Hadley said was the decision maker for Kellie, but she continued to think about it for a few minutes before she told him, "Let's just forget the camping for a while. I have a feeling I'll be able to do all I want once we get to Hulett, winter or spring."

Hadley smiled. "You have that right. Might even be able to get an igloo camping trip in. I have an igloo building tool in my gear, so it doesn't matter too much how much snow, or what kind of snow we get, I can still built a safe and secure one."

"Igloo, huh? I've never been in one." That started a long discussion of camping methods that consumed the time until Hadley pulled off the Interstate and they began to look for a restaurant before going to the motel where they were booked.

It went much the same the rest of the trip to Los Angeles. Kellie drove for a while several times, on the interstate sections of the trip, to get a feel for the Suburban and trailer. It was a bit difficult at first and she knew she was red as a beet more than once as she was getting the hang of the accelerator, clutch, and transmission gear shift.

But Hadley never said a discouraging or disparaging word, simply offering a little constructive advice a couple of times. He let her learn at her own pace. And soon enough she was handling the Suburban and trailer more than well enough.

They took five days and four nights for the trip and arrived rested. Their first stop for Kellie was at the mail service where her mail redirect was done.

She'd called before they left St. Louis to have them hold anything that came in while they were on the road. There wasn't much, but what there was of importance was quite a surprise.

"Well, Kellie said, sitting in the Suburban, reading the letter that was in the packet from Stringer News Network. "Seems like there is someone at SNN that didn't get the word I am persona non grata. Besides the standard COBRA insurance offer, which I think I will take until I get some other insurance, and the 401(k) rollover paperwork, there are three checks.

"One for three months full salary, one a very nice bonus check for the scoops, and one covering accumulated vacation and sick leave. That one isn't much."

"If I might make a suggestion?" Hadley asked.

"Sure! What?"

"You might want to carry more cash than usual. And in order to get it with the fewest hassles, I think if you deposit the checks in your account, you can write me a check for cash, and I'll give you the currency. Won't have to jump through any loopholes that way."

Kellie looked thoughtful. "I already do carry quite a bit of cash. Stashed all through my gear, just in case we have trouble on a shoot somewhere. But I guess it would be a good idea to double that. Or more.

"Hmm… And the bank is kind of finicky about deposit wait times and things like that. Doing it your way would certainly be easier." She looked over at Hadley. "Are you sure you…"

Hadley smiled and shook his head. "Wouldn't have suggested it if I wasn't willing to do it."

Kellie smiled back. "Yeah. Guess so. Okay. I'll do it that way. Should save us a full day. What say we get some lunch, on me, and then go get my things?"

"Plan A. I like it," Hadley replied and put the Suburban in gear.

Kellie was surprised after lunch when Hadley pulled into a U-Haul rental place. "Your trailer is plenty large enough for my things, Hadley. I don't have much furniture, at all."

Hadley grinned over at her. "My trailer isn't empty. Far from it. We'll need at least a small one for some of your things. Probably be easier to just get one large enough for all your stuff and not get into mine at all."

"Oh. I thought you just brought an empty trailer."

"Just goes to show how well she pulls, and how well the Suburban pulls it. Hard to tell it is loaded. Except for hard braking and you didn't have to do any of that while you were driving."

"I'm not sure I can handle two trailers, Hadley."

"Don't worry. You'll be fine on the open road. I'll handle any place that you aren't comfortable with, as well as my regular schedule."

Kellie looked a little doubtful. "Well… If you think so…"

Hadley pulled around on the lot into a position to make it easy to get to the trailer he thought they would need. As soon as Kellie got out of the Suburban she hurried to the rear of Hadley's trailer. Sure enough, there was a platform hitch as part of the bumper. She hadn't noticed it before.

A salesman was headed their way as Hadley opened the rear doors of the trailer he had his eye on. "What do you think? Take it all?"

"With room to spare. Well... I think so. I forgot about the prep stuff I bought recently. But... Yeah. I think so."

"And there is some room still in mine." He turned to the salesman. "We need this one. For a one-way to Wyoming."

"With which vehicle, sir?" asked the clerk. He looked around.

"The Suburban. It'll be the rear trailer of the two."

"I'm not sure..." the clerk stammered.

Calmly, Hadley said, "Check it out with your guys. I'll get the hitch out. I'll need it for a trailer from some rental place."

"Yes. Yes. I'll check. Be right back."

Hadley opened a locked tool box that was part of the fenders on the trailer and took out the square tube mount with the appropriate ball for the rental trailer. He had it installed and locked when the clerk and the store manager came back out.

Kellie stood back and admired Hadley's skill in getting the manager to agree to the rental. He'd never rented out a trailer as a second one; though they did get in trailers on one-way bring backs that were doubled sometimes. So he knew it could be done.

When Hadley headed in to do the paperwork, Kellie looked at her watch. Less than fourteen minutes since they'd arrived. "He's good," Kellie muttered. "I think I'd just better watch myself a little closer, if he turns that charm on around me. I'll be doing things I want to think about some more first."

But Kellie was smiling broadly when she followed Hadley and the clerk inside. She'd realized that she wouldn't have to watch it. Hadley had made it clear those subjects were off limits for the moment. It was going to be interesting when the time came for the discussions.

She paid for the trailer, still smiling, as the two men went back outside to hook it up.

CHAPTER EIGHT

Hadley kept the speed down with the second trailer once it was loaded. They had needed to put several cases of #10 canned freeze dried foods in Hadley's trailer so the rental would be balanced properly. But once Hadley had a feel for the train, he was just as comfortable as before.

Kellie was a bit intimidated, but Hadley handled it the way he had the first time she drove the Suburban. She went even slower than Hadley and only on the long straight stretches of interstate. Hadley did all the through city and mountain driving, and whenever they ran into snow.

With the speeds down, it took five days to get to the Lodge. Kellie realized he'd left more than a few details out of the description of the place.

Like the large two story log home, three other cottages, some out buildings, all in addition to the large log construction Lodge building. The place was a show case, the grass areas already showing some green, and the gravel drives and concrete paths kept clean.

She was in need of a pit stop and hurried into the Lodge when Hadley told her where the nearest bathroom was. Hadley pulled the rig around to where they would unload it into the house and used a bathroom himself there.

Kellie found him stacking her gear from the second trailer on the back porch of the house and began to help. "I take it I'm not staying in the Lodge." There was a hint of a question there.

"No. Paying customers only. You're my guest. You get one of the house guest rooms. I think you'll be comfortable."

"Oh. Okay. I'm not going to argue. I saw the list of services and pricing. This place must pay pretty good."

"Told you," Hadley said with a grin.

When the trailer was unloaded, Hadley moved it out of the way and unhooked it before going back to help Kellie again. He found her talking to Marissa Holland, the housekeeper for the house.

"I have the room ready, Hadley," Marissa told him when he joined the two. Sean and Elizabeth are coming over to move the things upstairs."

"We could have done that," Hadley said. He noticed that Kellie looked a little relieved. She was looking up the long staircase to the second floor. The house had ten foot ceilings on the first floor.

"There's an elevator," Hadley told Kellie with a smile.

"Oh. Then yes, we could have..."

"You're still a guest," Marissa said. "We'll take care of things like this until that changes."

Hadley introduced Kellie to Sean and Elizabeth. She was amazed at the size of the two. Sean was a wiry middle aged man, barely five foot seven. Elizabeth, on the other hand stood a full six foot two and probably weighed in at two hundred well-proportioned pounds.

"Our two wranglers," Hadley said as they picked up loads, as did Marissa, and disappeared around behind the stair case.

Kellie and Hadley took boxes and headed that way, too. They had to wait for the elevator, as the other three were already on the way up. "I noticed that Marissa said, guest until that changes." But she was smiling.

"Yep. Until that changes. I'm hoping it does, but that is for when the time comes to discuss it. For right now, I just want you safe and sound and able to take a step back and look at things. What you are going to do based on what is happening in the country and world."

It was a little intense, but Kellie kept smiling. She was already beginning to make some decisions. And Hadley was involved in at least some of them.

Halfway expecting the same décor as the Lodge, Kellie found the bedroom pleasantly modern, rather than rustic and outdoorsy. The bedroom was large, with a walk in closet and ensuite bathroom, also of a nice size.

"We'll handle the rest," Hadley insisted when everything from the porch was upstairs in Kellie's room. He and Kellie went back out to Hadley's trailer and proceeded to use the same handcart to unload the food boxes as they'd used to load them. Then went down a ramp into the basement through an outside access hatch.

"Why don't you see what you can score us for lunch," Hadley told Kellie after securing his trailer. "I'm going to unhook my trailer and hook the rental back up. I want to get it turned in. That thing is costing you an arm and a leg."

"Okay. I am getting hungry."

An hour later, filled to the gills with food, Hadley and Kellie were headed into the nearest U-Haul place to drop off the trailer. It took the rest of the afternoon. They didn't get back until almost nine.

A light supper was ready for them and then they went to their rooms, relaxing fully for the first time since Kellie had been so rudely fired.

For a week Hadley showed Kellie around the place, got her accustomed to riding the horses, shooting and showed her every detail of the operation, as well as the preps that were an integral part of the way things were set up. They were snowed in for three days at one point, and Kellie got a firsthand look at how the staff managed it easily.

Hadley, not one to miss scoring at least a few good points, could tell that Kellie was getting restless and asked her to sit her down after breakfast one morning to have a talk with her.

"Kellie, though I could extend the leave of absence, I don't think I need to do so. How do you feel about staying on here as part of the operation for a while longer, until you decide what you want to do?"

"Oh, Hadley! I've not given a single thought to you and that you might need to go back to work. I've just been having such a great time... I'm sorry."

"Don't be sorry, Kellie. I've enjoyed the time with you, too. But you aren't ready for anything more, yet and I know you need something to keep you busy. I suspect you won't want to stay here. But I wanted to make the offer."

"Oh. Well, thank you, Hadley! That is so sweet!" Kellie fell silent and looked down at her hands in her lap. She sighed finally and looked up to meet Hadley's even gaze. "And you're right. I'm not ready for more between us. I thought I'd give in, out of gratitude, but I haven't and know enough about myself now to know I won't. There are still too many unresolved things going on for me to think about settling down and starting a family.

"Even besides this potential problem, I still have the need to learn and investigate things. I need to get back to work, too, as a practical matter. But I'd like it to be as a reporter again. If anyone will have me. I have been too afraid to check on my reputation to see if it is even possible for me to get hired by anyone."

Hadley smiled. "That is so much part of why I care about you, Kellie. You don't give up and do what you think is right. I'm sure the local paper would take you on. But you are far more qualified than they need. So it is simply a matter of finding you a position befitting your abilities."

Kellie laughed lightly. "With you on my PR team, how can I not? But yes. I would take about anything, if they've ruined my reputation, but I know I can still do the tough stories. That's what I aim to do, I just realized. Even right along the lines of what we were doing, but without some of the political correctness I let creep into the segments."

"Good for you. St. Louis has several good stations that often have stories get on the big networks. It would be a place to start. And you'd have my place to fall back on there, or here, if there was any trouble. I'm sure you would want your own apartment, but the estate would be at your full disposal for use as a base."

"You'd do that for me? Even though..."

"Yes, I would. I am convinced you'll come around to my way of thinking eventually, and you are worth the wait."

"Oh, Hadley! You do make it tough sometimes. I hate the thought of just taking everything back to Missouri, but I guess, if you don't mind, I think I'd like to start there. Having a fallback position feels like a really good idea, still."

"Kellie, I don't see any point in you taking anything anywhere at the moment. You're still in good shape financially..."

"Thanks to you," Kellie interjected. "You haven't let me pay for anything out here."

"Yeah. Well. It's not like you're a draw on the expenses. But the point is, we could just go back, you could get a furnished apartment, which you'd have to do anyway, and then see about finding a reporting job in or around St. Louis. I'd be taking the trailer back, and between it and the Suburban; there'd be plenty of room to take back what you did want to have with you."

Hadley paused a second, but then added. "I'd just do a good selection of preps, to keep you comfortable, but be ready to come out to the estate for anything serious."

Kellie was looking thoughtful, and Hadley knew that she was weighing what he'd suggested carefully. Finally she smiled. "You do make good plans. That does sound doable. I'd have to get a vehicle, too..."

"I might even be able to help with that," Hadley said, not sure just how Kellie would take what he was going to suggest.

"You are not going to buy me a car!"

"No. More of a loaner until you get set again. I have a project in the works. It's been on a back burner with my mechanic, but it wouldn't take much to have it finished by the time we get back. It is something you could use for a while. Shake the bugs out of it for me."

"What kind of project?" Kellie asked, suddenly envisioning another Suburban. She liked it. But it wasn't her first choice in vehicles.

Her heart fell when Hadley said, "Something kind of like my Suburban." But she perked up when he continued. "But not nearly as big. Not quite as capable, either, and not armored. At least not the body. It is one of the early four door Jeep Wrangler Saharas.

"The owner blew the engine and transmission not long after he got it. I bought it then, with the intention of doing some modifications. My mechanic has been working on it since, as he had time. He called me recently and asked about finishing it up and getting it off his property. His business has picked up and he needs the space.

"You'd be doing him, and me, a favor by using it and giving us some feedback on changes and improvements and such."

"I don't know, Hadley. A Jeep sounds nice. I've always kind of wanted one, but this sounds a little too convenient."

"Well, maybe a little. But I think it would work for you. Some of the changes I wanted are in a removable rear box kind of thing. You wouldn't really need them and we could build a box to handle your reporting gear. Cameras, sound gear, and such, in case you go free-lance or have to work solo or with just one other person."

Kellie straightened up and her eyes sparkled. She had actually thought about free-lance work. But her preferred medium was video, and that was more difficult to do solo. She'd still have to get the equipment... Unless she got on with a station and they provided...

"Hmm. That does sound kind of intriguing, Hadley."

"It would just be until you are in the big leagues again and can get just what you want."

"What say we go back, and take a look at it and then I'll decide. This is on the edge of what I'm comfortable with."

"That's okay, Kellie. I understand. I'll call Mark here in a few minutes and make sure it is ready when we get back."

"But what if I decide not to use it?" Kellie asked.

"I still need to pick it up. I'll be getting it anyway."

"Oh. Okay. I guess that is the plan, then."

Hadley didn't push the time frame. Kellie seemed to want to take a day or two to say good-byes and thank Marissa and the entire Lodge staff for, as she put it, "Putting up with me."

But the Suburban was loaded up by noon on the second day, and the trailer attached to it. There'd been no need to put any of Kellie's things she was taking in the trailer. There was even room left in the back of the Suburban.

Hadley still had several days on the initial request for the leave of absence, so they took it easy again going to Missouri. They were stopping in Kansas City early one evening when the hands free cell phone in the Suburban rang.

Hadley looked over at Kellie when he answered the hands-free and it was Justin. The surprise was evident in her eyes, when Kellie said, "Justin! Are you okay? I didn't think you were supposed to be talking to me."

"I'm not, Kellie. But don't worry. I'm on a secure phone. And I have doubts they are monitoring anyway. Especially Hadley's phone in the Subaru. Glad I caught you. I was just going to see if he could get a message to you.

“We’re not…” Kellie was saying, intending to tell Justin about the Suburban, but Hadley quickly shook his head. “Never mind. What message did you need to get to me?”

“Things are heating up, Kellie. I’ve been spooking the spooks a little.”

“Oh, Justin! You’ll get hurt! Or in trouble!”

“Naw. I’m being careful. I can’t do anything about it. I don’t know if you can or not, but I thought you ought to know. The piece of information I got ahold of is that DHS isn’t really trying to stop the attack. They plan to take advantage of it in some way. Let a lot of people die, protecting only those that are supporting them. A major take over in the government when the time comes.

“I don’t want to push it, so I’m going to get off this phone. I just wanted to give you a heads up. And if you do decide to do anything, if there is anything that can be done, and I’m not convinced there is, be very careful. People are going to die, one way or another.

“And Kellie, don’t trust Carla. She’s sold out to DHS.

“You should have Hadley go over prepping in more detail with you. The rest of us have been digging into it and are trying to be ready for when this thing gets really bad. Good-bye. Bye, Hadley. Take good care of her if she’ll let you. She’s worth having around during this.”

“Oh, Justin!” Kellie said, coloring slightly. But there was dead air. Justin had hung up.

Kellie looked over at Hadley. "You didn't want me to tell him we're not in the Subaru?"

"No. The fewer people that know about this phone the better. The phone in the Subaru is re-directed to the Suburban."

"Oh. Clever!"

"Yeah. Expensive though. Hmm."

Hadley pulled into the hotel parking lot where they were staying the night. He stopped at the entrance and got out of the Suburban. As Kellie joined him, Hadley quietly said, "Whatever you decide, I've got your back on this."

Kellie glanced at Hadley, but there was a crowd in the reception area and she didn't want to discuss it in public.

CHAPTER NINE

It was over a quiet dinner at one of Kansas City's steak houses that Kellie brought it up later that evening.

"You think what I'm planning could be physically dangerous, don't you, Hadley?"

Hadley nodded his eyes on hers. "I do. For a variety of reasons. Not just our government, or, more accurately I'm sure, elements within our government. But also even Allah's Warriors, if it becomes obvious you are working, not to spread the word, but how to avoid the problems if they succeed."

Kellie paled. It was hard to tell in the softly lighted restaurant, but Hadley noticed. "I'm not trying to scare you off the project. I just want you to be aware of the dangers. And that I'll being doing my best to prevent anything happening to you."

Kellie nodded. "I'm not going to let it go. I can't."

Hadley nodded. "I fully understand."

Kellie looked thoughtful for a moment and changed the subject when she spoke. "I wonder what Justin meant about Carla? She's been my staunchest supporter at SNN."

"How sure are you of that?" Hadley asked. "If you'll note, she was the one that apologized on your behalf for airing the segment about the dangers of the fungal infestations."

"I figure she had to do that," Kellie said slowly. "I mean, she's been so supportive since I first applied. There was even some talk of me becoming her protégé at some point, once I proved myself. I never gave the rumors much credence, but they did exist."

"I haven't known Justin very long," Hadley replied after taking a sip of wine, "But I don't think he'd bring it up without a good reason."

"That's true," Kellie said, still looking thoughtful. "But probably a moot point. I can't see any chance of Carla and I having any interaction in the future."

"Well, if it does come up, just keep what Justin said in mind. You feel like dessert?"

Kellie sighed and smiled at Hadley. "Can I have a bite or two of yours? I think I'm gaining weight with all the good cooking I've been exposed to lately."

Hadley chuckled. "Of course. And you aren't gaining weight. You look fabulous."

"Maybe three bites then?" Kellie laughed. And Hadley noted that she didn't mention the compliment.

It took most of the next day to get to Hadley's Missouri estate. Due to a near blizzard, there was a bad accident on the Interstate and traffic was held up for several hours.

Hadley also noted that Kellie agreed without argument to stay at the estate until she found an apartment, rather than spend the money on a hotel. Her trust in him made him even more firm in his conviction to let Kellie set the pace for their relationship, if any such developed further than the friendship they now had.

The bad weather hit St. Louis that night and Kellie, despite her eagerness, decided to not try and get out looking for an apartment. She spent most of the day on the internet looking for one, however, and checking on the local TV stations for possible job opportunities.

She also took the few minutes Hadley needed to show her the rest of the preps at the estate, including the roomy, comprehensive underground shelter that was between the house and the unattached garage, connected to each with tunnels.

Hadley spent the day catching up on class assignments and talking to his substitute that covered for him when he was gone on one of his occasional leaves. He also checked with Mark Austin about the Jeep.

But on Wednesday, using the Subaru again, Hadley took Kellie in to Austin's Garage to take a look at the Jeep Wrangler Sahara. She was in love the instant she saw it. Sort of a gold color, which surprised her, it was well equipped she discovered, but not to the degree the Suburban was.

And Hadley was right about the space behind the rear seats. It would be perfect for camera and sound equipment. And with the rear seats folded down there was even more room.

Like the Suburban, the Jeep had a front rack with spare tire, winch, hitch, tow bar, and some pioneer tools. A rear rack equipped similarly, with extra fuel cans. And the roof rack with gear, lights, fixed and fold down antennas, was also similar to the Suburban. Just not nearly as big or as much gear.

Even the dash in the Jeep was similar to the Suburban, with built in faraday cages for all the electronics. And it was a diesel, which in retrospect, she should have guessed. A Cummins 4BT non-electronic with a manual transmission.

She spotted the radiator armor and Hadley told her that there was some armor in a few key places to protect the driver, but the Jeep wasn't armored in the sense the Suburban was. When she fired up the Cummins she realized that it, like the 6BT in the Suburban, was well muffled and otherwise quieted down so the diesel rattle was minimal.

"I hate to say it," Kellie said after taking the Jeep on a short run, "but I do want to use it, Hadley. It is a great rig."

Hadley smiled. "Sure thing. I thought you would. Once you get something semi-permanent or better, we'll replace the custom cargo box in the back with one set up for your specific needs."

"That's not..." But the calm look Hadley gave her caused her words to trail off. "Well, okay. But I'll pay... help pay for that."

Hadley smiled. "The license and insurance is good for another month, but I'll get it added to my other vehicles after school today. So, for now, I guess you are on your own for the day."

"Thank you, Hadley," Kellie said. She stepped up and gave him a quick peck on the cheek. "You treat me too well."

Hadley found he couldn't say anything, so he just nodded. But then he was able to say, calmly, "You take off and I'll finish up with Mark and get to the college."

A light feeling in his heart, Hadley watched the grinning Kellie take off in the Jeep, merging with traffic on the street expertly. Her experiences in the Suburban had her working the diesel engine and manual transmission like a champ already.

"Well, old son," said Mark, "finally got that thing out of my hair. She the one, you think?"

"What?"

"She… That woman… She the one you're going to marry?"

"We'll see, Mark. We'll see. Now let's figure up the totals so I can get to school and save my job."

"Bah! They'll never let you go. Especially after that news show you were on. It's the buzz around here. Upped my preps quite a bit because of it. So have a bunch of the others."

"That's good. So have I," Hadley said. He followed Mark into the garage office.

Kellie was waiting for Hadley at the estate when he got home that evening. Without a word she had him in a hard hug. She stepped back, turned a little red, but quickly said. "Sorry. But this has been the best day! That Jeep is a dream. And a little magic, I think.

"Found a great apartment, and even got offered two jobs, one of which I will take! And freelance the other. If I can swing that, anyway. All in the span of a few hours.

"The one job comes with a camera person. I don't know if she is as good as Justin, but from what I saw, she is very good. We really hit it off. And my soon to be producer is gung-ho about doing some more of the preparedness stories, along with everything else."

Kellie smiled and a bit more calmly said, "All thanks to you, Hadley. You've been good for me, as well as to me."

"All your own doing," Hadley said. "And I have good news, too. I get to keep my job."

Kellie looked startled. And then worried. "You said there wouldn't be a problem!"

Hadley smiled. "There wasn't. I just always feel that way when I come back from one of my leaves. One of these days they are just going to tell me to not come back. But that is in the future. Far future, I hope. But in the meantime, I'm not going to have much free time.

"The school, not me, got a contract to do in-depth research on combatting the fungal diseases for the government."

"Justin said DHS didn't want to try to stop it," Kellie said.

"I know. It is probable the right hand doesn't know what the left hand is doing. Or it will just be a sham effort so they look like they are doing something constructive. I'll be able to tell once I get in on it. They've already got some things set up and running.

"But don't worry. We'll get you moved and set up tomorrow. I don't actually start until Friday."

"That's great, Hadley. Thanks. So. What do you want for supper? I thought I'd try my hand in the kitchen. You do have a day to recover."

Hadley laughed.

A very tired Kellie came back out to the estate on Saturday to fill Hadley in on what had transpired on Thursday and Friday, and to pick up an order of preps she'd had sent to the estate since she wouldn't be home to accept it.

She used the key that Hadley had given her early on, and finally found him in his isolation lab and greenhouse, set off alone on the property. The front door was unlocked, and she went in. She could see him moving around inside the actual lab area, surrounded by growing plants, and all kinds of equipment.

He was suited up in an environmental protective suit with respirator, gloves, and everything else to avoid contaminating what was in the lab, so he could decontaminate easily and not carry anything out of the lab when he left.

Kellie knocked on the thick glass and Hadley looked over. She couldn't see him smile broadly, due to the respirator, but he waved immediately and went over to an intercom box on the wall.

Seeing what he was doing, Kellie looked around and found a similar box on her side of the glass and went over to it. Between the respirator and the intercom, he was a bit hard to understand, but she finally figured out that he would be out in about an hour and for her to make herself at home.

So Kellie nodded and waved, and went back to the house. It would be just enough time to put together a lunch for them.

Hadley was able to watch her working in the kitchen for a couple of minutes before she saw him. Both smiled. "Feeding me again?" Hadley asked and took a seat at the kitchen serving counter.

"I thought I should, after all the meals you furnished. Besides, I need the practice. I haven't had to cook for myself for quite a while. Got to eating out, often, when I was so busy all the time."

"I understand. So, how are things going?"

Kellie handed Hadley a plate with a sandwich and wedge of lettuce, and then poured him a glass of freshly brewed iced tea. "You first. When I get started, I don't want to stop."

Hadley took a bite of the sandwich, made appropriate approval sounds, took a drink of the tea, and then said, "Meshing in with the team just fine. Seems to be legitimate work, but I won't know until I see how they handle some of the findings.

"I decided to do some work on my own here. Nothing to do with the fungal problem. I won't risk the contamination of my own growing plants by working with infected ones here.

"But I still maintain tight isolation to avoid any problems in the processing and testing. So if I'm a little adamant about not having you out there, it is nothing personal."

"I didn't even think, Handley! I'm sorry! I shouldn't have gone looking for you."

"It's alright. There shouldn't be any problems, as I'm very careful. But I want to do some additional fruit tree graftings for both estates. Just getting the lab set up today. Haven't used it for a couple of years.

"It just hit me that I might as well keep working on my own projects as well as the fungal one, and the lectures. Need to keep busy. But whenever you need me, I still have some flexibility. Trees don't grow in a day, and the work at the school lab is mostly sit and wait, too.

"This is a great sandwich. So, what is it you want to tell me without stopping?"

Kellie set the rest of her sandwich on her plate and launched into a detailed explanation of her activities the last two days. "It is even better than I thought Wednesday evening, Hadley!

"Pamela is good on the camera. A bit of a free spirit and willing to go for the hard shots. And Heather, my producer, is quiet, thoughtful, but very insightful. She'll let me take stories the direction I want, for the most part, as long as I don't get out of line.

"And the apartment is fine. I've got it all straightened out now. The Jeep is a dream. Pamela already wants to buy it, or one like it." Kellie laughed.

"When we took it by Austin's Garage after an assignment yesterday, and he quoted us a price for a slide in for reporting equipment, she asked him how much to have a Jeep set up like yours."

Kellie shook her head. "Hadley. Almost eighty-thousand dollars? And you're just letting me just use it?"

"Of course. Did Pamela order one?"

Kellie had to laugh. "No. She didn't. But she drooled for a while thinking about it. And I will be able to swing the box. I'll have to wait on some equipment, but it won't be long. I'm going to have Mark build it to fit what I eventually want, rather than what Pamela has now. Still work with her equipment, but I want some additional things."

Hadley nodded. "That is just what I wanted you to do. You want me to finance the..."

"No, Hadley. I'll get it as I can, on my salary.

"Now, I hate to eat and run, but I need to load up that delivery and get back to the apartment. We've got a story to cover tomorrow. Nothing earth shattering, but a good story, none the less. And I need to catch up on sleep. Friday was a long day."

"I saw the story. It was a good first one for you at the station." Hadley said.

Kellie could tell he meant it. She'd felt good about the story and it had showed. "Thanks."

"Don't worry about the dishes," Hadley said when Kellie started to clean up the kitchen. "Let's get those preps loaded and get you home to some rest. You want me to come in and help you unload?"

Kellie shook her head. "No. It is just those few cases. I can handle them okay."

Kellie came around out of the kitchen and stepped up to Hadley. She cupped his cheek with her right hand. "Thank you for all you've done, Hadley. Things are really working out."

Hadley smiled. He was still smiling when Kellie drove off in the golden Jeep.

CHAPTER TEN

The two didn't see each other much for over a month. Both were busy with their respective careers. And nothing untoward had happened concerning Kellie's new St. Louis based series on preparing for disasters, the first of which addressed the New Madrid Seismic Zone possibilities for major earthquakes in the area.

There was nothing, anywhere, being broadcast about the terrorist threat of releasing fungal infections into key US crops at planting time or shortly thereafter. And planting time was coming up.

Only on some prepper sites on the internet was the subject a hot topic. Kellie was building her preps, with most of them stored at Hadley's. One of the times that they did have together, Hadley took Kellie to the minimal bug-out location not too far away and helped her cache some supplies there for her use, in a bug out scenario.

The visit brought home the seriousness of some of the situations that Hadley made preparations to deal with, including some violent ones. Though Kellie couldn't see why anyone would want to take over the small concrete block building, when Hadley showed her the signs of hunters and druggies having used the place before, she was convinced.

And after the training on how to take it back over, preferably with non-lethal means, but also last ditch lethal means, she realized he would protect what was his. That probably included her. Whether she was ready for it or not, he would take care of her.

Kellie was thoughtful on the ride back to her apartment that Sunday. She realized that if push came to shove, she would willingly allow it. She just wasn't sure if she could bring herself to harm others to protect herself. It never crossed her mind what she might do to protect Hadley. It was inconceivable that he would need protecting.

Another week later, with planting of the threatened crops in full swing, Hadley was called out of a lecture class by one of the team working on solutions.

"Hadley, this is strange," said Caroline McQuiddy. She handed him a piece of paper with another college logo. Hadley looked it over. It was a request for fairly large fungal samples for the college to do testing on their own, at the behest of DHS.

It sent a shiver down Hadley's back. There were three misspelled words, and the logo on the letterhead page was just not very clear. And the request was marked urgent.

Hadley asked, coming to a quick conclusion of what he would do, "Who has seen this?"

"Just me. It was in the regular mail. I didn't know what to do about it when I opened it up. Should we pull the samples and send them off, or let someone in purchasing or administration or something do it?"

"Don't worry about it. I'll take care of this," Hadley told Caroline. "Can't just be giving away our livelihood, now can we? Urgent, huh?" Hadley forced what he considered a rather weak chuckle.

Caroline took it as the joke he was trying to make. "Just don't get DHS down on us." She laughed. "And remember, time is relative."

"Absolutely," Hadley said. Caroline hurried back to the lab. Hadley walked slowly back to the lecture hall, thinking. It was all he could do to complete the lecture. But when it was over and he waded through half a dozen questions, he was finally able to get to his office.

He did a couple of quick checks online. "They have to be crazy," Hadley muttered. He made several copies of the request, and stashed one in the office. The original he put into one of the school logo envelopes and included a handwritten note about it being suspicious to him. He addressed the envelope simply DHS, Washington, DC. He added a stamp and slipped the envelope into his left hip pocket.

The other copies of the request he took out to the Subaru and dropped the envelope into the outgoing mail box on his way to the lab. There wasn't much really going on in the lab. They were waiting for some test results that wouldn't be ready until the next day. Everyone agreed, independently of Hadley, to make it an early day.

Hadley wasted no time getting home. He knew he was risking a lot, including possibly Kellie's life. But he called her cell phone on the way home and asked to come by her apartment after she got home.

She could hear the concern in his voice and quickly agreed. It would be late, but he was more than welcome to stop in.

Kellie was still in her on-camera clothes when Hadley rang the bell and she opened the door.

"Something is wrong, isn't it?" she asked immediately. "I could hear it in your voice on the phone."

"Yes. I think something is very wrong. And very dangerous." Hadley handed Kellie the last copy of the request.

"You've got to be kidding? Isn't it kind of late to be starting on research for this? Aren't you guys the lead agency for it?"

"Look at the logo. And check for typos," Hadley said.

Kellie looked at the document more closely. "Oh. You'd think a college would have a spell checker on their word processor. And professionally printed letterhead." Suddenly her eyes widened. "This is fake!"

"And why would someone fake a request to get deadly fungal samples in the middle of a threat to attack the US food supply with fungi?"

"Oh, my Lord! You think this is from the terrorists? You think they want us to supply the means to our own end? That's crazy!"

"But rather poetic, wouldn't you say?" Hadley replied.

Kellie turned away, lifted her left hand up and ticked her front teeth with her thumbnail, something she did when in deep thought. She spun back around. "What if this isn't the only request? What if they are asking everyone that might have spores."

"Possibly. But that would be very dangerous. The main thing is what do we do about it? I sent the original off to DHS on a slow boat to China, as my official response. Because I'm not sure we can trust them. We might have to handle this on our own."

"I'm not sure what we can do," Kellie said. "If I just do a report about the request, it could do more harm than good." Again she looked thoughtful. Hadley had an idea of what he wanted to do, but preferred it come from Kellie herself.

And he was glad he held back his own suggestion until she made hers. “We have this address in Kansas City,” Kellie said. “If we monitor the drop, and I’m sure that is what it is, we might be able to find out who is actually asking. It is not beyond the realm of possibility, at least in my mind, that the DHS could be behind this.”

“My thoughts exactly. But that isn’t something we can do ourselves, Kellie. Neither of us can just take off this time. Too much at stake. But I know a couple of PI types that could handle it, as long as they know the possibilities. Just to get us some names or a physical address.”

“I don’t know, Hadley. I’m willing to risk my own life. And I know I won’t talk you out of risking yours. But someone else? I don’t know if I could live with myself if someone dies because of something I do.”

“People, a lot of people, are going to die, if this isn’t stopped. Cold. It would only delay the attack if they don’t get the stuff from us. I can’t fathom that this is their Plan A, but it has fallen into our lap. They are bound to have alternate plans.”

“Very true. Okay. Give it to your buddy. But be very clear about the dangers.”

“Oh, that I will. And it will be impossible to keep him out of the action if it comes to something. It is hard for me to believe that this will lead us directly to the terrorists, but if it gives a lead that the DHS can’t ignore, then we might stop them anyway.”

Kellie watched as Hadley pulled out his cell phone, searched his contacts, and then made the call. It was very cryptic, and Kellie couldn’t imagine just what Hadley was actually telling the guy.

But when Hadley hung up, he asked her, "Can I use your internet and computer?"

"Yes. Of course," replied Kellie. Her computer was already connected and up.

"I alerted Sam to check his e-mail. I'll send him the details through my e-mail. We use an encryption system for things like this."

"Oh. That's good," Kellie said. She sat quietly while Hadley composed the message, encrypted it, and then sent it.

"You want some coffee while we wait?" Kellie asked.

"I probably should go," Hadley replied. "I can check my e-mail when I get home."

"Not on your life!" Kellie said. "I want to know as soon as you get it what the word is. You'll stay here all night if you have to."

"But..."

"No buts. You're staying until that e-mail comes through, or we have to get to work."

"Okay then," Hadley said. "Coffee it is."

Fortunately they didn't have to wait long. Hadley checked his e-mail every fifteen minutes. The third time he had the message. When he decoded it he showed it to Kellie.

"Understood. On it."

"That's all?" Kellie asked. "No questions or anything?"

"That is Sam. He doesn't waste words. As soon as he knows, he'll send me something. I promise to get it to you as quickly as possible. But for now, I need to head home."

"Okay. Thanks Hadley." Kellie walked him to the door and watched as he went down the hallway. "Should of kissed him," she suddenly thought to herself.

It was three anxious days before Hadley called Kellie again. He asked her to come out to his place this time after work.

She was able to leave a bit early and had to wait for Hadley to get home. Kellie was puttering in the kitchen when he came in.

"What'cha got?" she immediately asked him.

"An address," Hadley said. "They really screwed up, Sam said. Went directly from the mail drop to a safe house. Drove straight through. Sam said it had all the earmarks. Guess where it is?"

"Chicago?" Kellie said on a hunch.

Hadley looked surprised. "Yes."

"Right where it started. That's not so far that I can't go there and expose this myself," Kellie said.

Hadley nearly panicked. "You are not going to..."

"Hear me out, Hadley. If we set this up right, I can get a scoop, and get enough publicity to make sure it is followed through with, even if DHS doesn't really want to.

"But it is going to have to be a hands on operation. I have a plan forming. Give me till tomorrow evening to figure it all out."

"Oh, Kellie! I don't know. I don't want to lose you. This is going to be very dangerous, the closer we get to the center of it."

Again Kellie cupped Hadley's cheek. And this time she did kiss him. "I know," she said softly. "And I feel the same way about you. But this has to take precedence."

"Okay. Okay. But I'm there every step of the way."

Kellie nodded. "I'm counting on that. Now it is my turn to get home and do some thinking."

Reluctantly Hadley watched her go. She was a part of him now, no matter what, and he wasn't going to lose her. He got on the computer and started sending out some more encrypted e-mails.

Kellie called him the next afternoon. She sounded exasperated and disappointed. "The station wouldn't go for it on what I was willing to tell them," she told Hadley. "But Pamela is insisting on sticking with me if I decide to, as she put it, 'Go for whatever scoop you have scoped.' I'll never be able to convince her otherwise. And it is too dangerous for her."

"You're going to need a camera person. I was going to offer, but if she is willing, I might be able to set something up to protect all of us."

"What do you mean?"

"I contacted a few more prepper friends. I have a security team to go to meet us in Chicago. All you have to do is give the word when."

"It has to be right now, Hadley," Kellie said. "We could lose the whole ball of wax if we delay. Tomorrow to get there and scope it out, and do the deed Sunday."

"I'll let them know. Meet at the Museum of Natural History? Three in the afternoon?"

"I guess so." There was silence for a few moments. "Hadley?"

"Yes, Kellie?"

"I'm scared, Hadley."

"So am I, Kellie." He didn't tell her he was scared for her, not himself. "I'll meet you at your apartment at seven in the morning."

"Okay. Pamela and I will be ready."

Hadley spent the afternoon unloading vulnerable items from the top rack and front rack that might be destroyed by gunfire, and pretty much everything on the rear rack.

Kellie and Pamela both paled slightly when Kellie asked about the absence of the items on the racks and Hadley told them it was to avoid damage from gunfire. Something that might just happen.

Kellie and Pamela were amazed to see the group assembled at one of the parking lots for the Museum of Natural History that day at three.

"Hadley," Kellie whispered, "Do these people know just how illegal it is to have firearms here in the city?"

"Yes, they do. And only a couple of licensed people are carrying. Including Sam. The others are here to run interference. Now. What is the plan?"

"The plan?" Kellie asked, turning pale.

"You said you were thinking up a plan."

"Yeah. I did. And I did. But it kinda of seems lame now. And a lot more dangerous than I thought at first."

"Let's hear it," Hadley said gently.

"Okay. Once we check the place out today, tomorrow morning, we go there, announce ourselves, tell them we know who they are, and that we are reporting them to DHS. Make sure they see us with the cameras. When they come boiling out, we lead them on the most direct line to a police station."

Kellie looked like she was going to cry.

"That'll work," Hadley said. He looked over and when he saw Sam, motioned him over. "Sam, we're going to lead them right to the closest police station that can handle them. Can you get word that there might be something big going on in the morning?"

"Good plan. I was worried about having to take them on directly. Yep. I can get word to the right people. We ready to go take a look? Security here is getting antsy."

"Yep. You're in the lead," Hadley said. He looked at Kellie. "You and Pamela with me in the Suburban today and tomorrow. Get the gear."

"But..." Kellie said, looking over at her Jeep.

"No arguments, Kellie, or the whole plan is off."

"Okay. I guess that would be safer for us," Kellie admitted. "Let's get what we need for a drive by video," she told Pamela.

Hadley had liked Pamela when he met her that morning. She was very straight forward and looked to be quite capable. She didn't ask many questions, just followed along picking up what she needed at the moment, knowing she'd get the full story soon.

Everyone that Hadley had brought into the scheme had at least some convoy training and they were able to follow Sam and each other at discrete distances to the safe house and past without arising any suspicion from the terrorists or the local law enforcement.

They stopped at a convenient place and checked notes. Everyone had picked out a good spot to be when the thing started. It would be up to Hadley to get the terrorists to follow him in the Suburban, while the others blocked possible turn offs until they reached the police station.

The time was set, and everyone went their separate way to get hotels or motels on their own. Hadley took Kellie and Pamela back to get her Jeep and then they went to the hotel nearby.

No one was very hungry, and after a quiet discussion of what they would each be doing the next day, they all turned in fairly early. They would need to be up by five and on the way by six to get the best chance of having clear streets for the event.

CHAPTER ELEVEN

Kellie was dressed in her blue chambray shirt and the khaki pants she'd worn in Memphis, along with the leather jacket. It was a cold morning and she shivered a bit while Hadley let the Suburban warm up and they went over the plan one more time.

Kelly wasn't nearly as cold by the time Hadley had Pamela, and then her, in body armor, including Level IV rifle plates. She was relieved when Hadley then put on his own armor.

When they were ready, Kellie got into the rear passenger seat, behind Hadley. She would be on the side toward the house. Pamela would use the camera across Kellie's body when she didn't have it on Kellie's face.

Kellie had to start three times as Hadley drove slowly, with Pamela videoing her on-camera recital of what was happening. But she quickly had that calm demeanor in place and was explaining everything neatly and concisely before they got very far.

She finished up as Hadley turned onto the street where the safe house was. "And this is where it starts," Kellie said.

Hadley flipped four switches and there came four thunks as the tire armor chains deployed.

They weren't a minute too early getting there. Three men were loading a non-descript sedan with suitcases, and the package that Sam had salted with harmless fungi before putting in the mail drop. It made it almost too easy.

Hadley stopped the Suburban, Pamela had the camera going through the window beside Kellie and Kellie opened the door and put one foot on the ground.

"We know you are Allah's Warriors! We know you have the fungi! We are making a citizen's arrest! Drop any weapons and..."

Kellie didn't waste any time. They didn't drop their weapons. They pulled them. From waistbands and from the car. A dozen shots slammed into the Suburban, but Hadley had it in gear. As soon as Kellie's foot was inside he gunned it. But not too hard.

He gave the terrorists time to get into the sedan and pull out after them. Hadley let them get a couple of more shots off, that hit the rear armor glass. Pamela had slipped into the rear of the Suburban and flinched when one of the rounds hit right where her camera was pointing. Except for the armor glass, the bullet would have gone through the camera and into her eye.

But as Kellie gave a running account, crouched on the rear seat of the Suburban, and Pamela continued to video the car behind them, Hadley kept going. More slowly than Kellie had expected. Bullets were pounding the rear of the Suburban. But there was nothing on the rear rack to be damaged, except the rack itself, and the sheet metal and armor glass of the rear doors.

As they came to each intersection, there would be a vehicle turned across the side street to block the terrorists from bugging out of the chase and getting away.

The terrorists were so intent on stopping the Suburban it was some time before they recognized that they were being herded. Twice they tried to ram past a blocking vehicle, but they were all large vehicles, and like the Suburban, had stout racks on the front bumpers that pushed the sedan back into the chase.

Hadley suddenly sped up significantly. They were coming up to the police station. They would have to make a turn there. Sam and the other armed man were there blocking the through street with two more large vehicles, to force the terrorists to turn as well.

Whoever Sam had contacted had taken heed of the warning. Dozens of heavily armed Chicago Police were lined up behind barriers when Hadley slid to a stop, throwing Pamela and Kellie around a bit as he twisted the wheel to bring the front of the Suburban to face the on rushing sedan.

"Brace yourselves!" Hadley called out, doing so himself.

But the terrorist driving thought better of the idea of ramming into the heavy front rack of the Suburban. And the other two quickly threw down their weapons and stepped out of the car when ordered to do so.

Kellie was already out, with Pamela on her heels, camera up. Kellie talked quickly but calmly, and she and Pamela got everything they could before the Police could stop them.

Hadley handed one of the Officers a printed statement and ushered Kellie and Pamela back into the Suburban and took off before they could be detained. Hadley retracted the tire armor to avoid quite as much interest that it might draw to the Suburban.

"They are going to try to charge us with some crimes," Hadley told Kellie and Pamela. "But I'll take the brunt of it. I have a good criminal lawyer on retainer. Might get a slap on the wrist, but since I was driving, and leading them on, I should be the only one to get into trouble. If you just let me handle it."

"That's fine with me," Pamela said. She was checking the equipment, half terrified she might have screwed something up. But everything was good and she finally sighed in relief.

Kellie wanted to argue the point, but left it when Hadley gave her one of those looks that brooked no argument.

They stopped long enough to group together and make sure no one was hurt and that none of the vehicles were too damaged to get home.

There was damage to the rear brake, turn signal, back up, and running lights, on the Suburban, but the fixtures were all aftermarket LED units, and at least some of the LEDs in each fixture were working, so there wasn't much likelihood of being stopped for no brake lights.

None of the other vehicles had taken a single round.

With assurances that everything was fine, everyone headed their separate ways, with the police none the wiser of any of their participation in the event.

A quick stop at the hotel, to put the raw footage up on the internet and then pick up Kellie's Jeep and the three main participants were on the way back to St. Louis. It was barely nine o'clock.

Hadley was towing the Jeep, keeping Kellie and Pamela in the Suburban, just in case there was another terrorist that might be following. But after many twists and turns and a very roundabout route to get there, they were at Hadley's that afternoon with no sign of a tail.

"You guys are staying here for a few days," Hadley told the two women in no uncertain terms. "I can protect you here for a few days until this settles down. And if we do have to go anywhere, and I stress the 'WE'. it'll be in the Suburban and I'll be carrying like I usually do."

Pamela kept quiet. She wasn't adverse to the security, but was curious how Kellie would handle the instructions. She was a little surprised when Kellie didn't take off on Hadley, but she only protested quietly, once, and let it go at that.

Hadley had Kellie take Pamela down to the shelter and get her settled in and asked Kellie to set up down there, as well, while he stayed topside to keep an eye on things.

"Put your cellular next to the cellular antenna at the comms desk," Hadley told Kellie. "It's already ungrounded and ready to go. You'll be getting calls, I'm sure, and can get a signal if you stay close to the antenna wire."

Both women had chances to take showers and get something to eat before the calls started. And Pamela got her share from the station. She referred them all to Kellie. Let her take the abuse. Pamela was camera; Kellie was the voice and image.

Hadley came down a bit later, sheepishly hooked up a laptop and got them on the internet, with video Skype capability. Kellie didn't get to bed until after midnight.

Hadley didn't get much sleep either, worried about there being more terrorists, primarily, but also that certain DHS personnel might take it personally.

Kellie called him on the intercom the next morning shortly after six. "Hadley, we have some breakfast ready down here."

"Okay. I could use some. I'll be right down."

"Everything okay up top?" Pamela asked when Hadley came into the shelter.

Hadley nodded. “No sign of anything.”

“Hadley,” Kellie said, “I’m not going to be able to stay sequestered very much longer. I have several offers over the internet to do something on the story live. The station is adamant that we keep it exclusive to them. And even SNN wants me back. Marcy called and essentially begged.”

“A lot to think about,” Hadley said, taking the plate of scrambled eggs and toast Kellie handed him. “I’m still worried about repercussions...”

“I’m willing to give it today,” Kellie replied. “But tomorrow I have to get back on this. I don’t want to lose momentum. And you need to get to work. I just hope the school doesn’t fire you over this.”

“I think I’ll be fine. But I prefer to stay here and...”

“We’re okay down here,” Kellie said. “As long as you think you will also be safe, going to work will be good for you. I suspect you didn’t get much sleep. Going to work might let you rest better than here.”

Kellie chuckled when Hadley smiled. “You could be right.” Hadley thought it over for a few moments as he wolfed down the food. “Yes. Okay. I’ll go in. Monitor the place from down here. If something does come up notify me on the internet. I’ll keep my phone ready for internet use.”

Kellie nodded.

“And under no circumstances leave here unless I give you an all clear.”

Again Kellie nodded. “If you would, go by my apartment and see if it is being staked out. I need to decide how to go about getting back in touch.”

It was Hadley’s turn to nod. “Okay. Then I’m going to head in.”

Kellie and Pamela watched Hadley leave. “He’s really distracted,” Kellie told Pamela.

“He’s scared for you. And me, too, of course, but mostly for you. And just so you know, I’m with you on this all the way.”

“Thanks Pamela.” Kellie went to the computer and got back on the internet to learn what she could about the situation. Pamela monitored the surveillance systems for the estate.

Hadley did actually work in a couple of short naps between classes and lab work that day. But he headed home as soon as he could. He’d heard a lot of comments about Kellie’s report. No one at the school realized he had been part of it, though several asked if he knew anything about it, since he’d been her expert for the show that one time.

He could find no evidence of anyone doing surveillance at Kellie’s apartment.

Feeling a little better, Hadley tensed up when he drove up to the garage at the estate. There was a black Suburban parked there, with two men in suits that screamed DHS standing beside it, smoking.

“Mr. Robertson,” said one of the men, straightening up from his leaning position against their Suburban. Both men looked cold due to the blustery wind blowing. Both flashed DHS identification. “We’d like to talk to you. In confidence.”

"About what?"

The other man managed a small smile. "I suspect you know, but not in what context." He looked around. "Can we go inside?"

"I am specifically not giving you permission to do a search without a warrant."

"We're not here for that, Mr. Robertson," said the first man, Agent Harris.

"Okay. But be aware that I will defend myself against illegal actions."

"Boy, Justin was right. This one is a tiger," said the second agent, Mathews.

Only when they were inside did Harris pull a rather large packet of papers from his inside jacket pocket. "I think you need to see these. Get them to Manson."

Hadley thumbed through the papers, expecting to see a list of charges or a request to come in for questioning. Instead, what he found were copies of various notes, memos, and printouts of some very interesting things.

"We're not willing to come forward on this," Mathews said. "But we are also not willing to let some people in the service get by with what they've been doing. If she thinks she can do anything about it she is free to use the information any way to take down those responsible for this."

"You mentioned a Justin?" Hadley asked after looking at the papers a second time, more thoroughly this time.

"Manson's former camera person. Some of those came from him. About the media involvement. He's lucky it was the two of us assigned to check out his report. We squelched it, because some of these people play plenty rough. He'll get himself killed if he isn't careful. What do you think?"

Both agents looked at Hadley expectantly.

"I'll get this to Kellie when I find her. Let her decide what to do. But one thing. I won't be pleased if this is some kind of set up."

"Don't threaten us," Mathew's said firmly. "We're still DHS and do not have to put up with it."

"Yeah. Right," Hadley said, but shut up before he really antagonized the two agents. "And there is no way you'll back this up on camera?"

"Not a chance," Harris said. "We have families to protect."

Hadley waited as long as he thought Kellie could stand it before he quit watching for other agents and went down to the shelter.

"DHS?" Kellie asked, looking a little pale.

Pamela told Hadley, "They showed up about half an hour before you got here and did some looking around. But they didn't try to get into any of the buildings or anything. Couldn't raise you on the internet."

"They want me for crimes or questioning?" Kellie asked after taking a quick, deep breath.

"Neither," Hadley said. He handed her the packet of papers. "Take a look at these. You'll have a hard time believing it. Some of it is from Justin."

"Yeah," Kellie said, surprising Hadley no end. "He e-mailed me this one. Said he just couldn't let it go. Carla has been working with some DHS people to disseminate disinformation about the situation. Along with several other major media people.

"And some of this implicates high level DHS people." Kellie looked up at Hadley. "I have to get this out, somehow, risk or no risk."

"I know," Hadley said. "Any thoughts on how to do that?"

"Yes, she does," Pamela said. "Crazy ones."

"What does Pamela mean?" Hadley asked Kellie.

"Just that I want to pull another fast one. Initially on SNN, but now on DHS, too. Just do a broadcast, with all this laid out. Oh. And I did get a lot more about the terrorists. Chicago PD made a couple of statements that I caught on the internet.

"Seems the terrorists are singing like canaries. They couldn't get the fungi from the source they had a deal with. Died in an auto accident, just by chance. They came up with the hair-brained scheme to get it from the school after they couldn't find any other sources."

"Ah. You'd work all that into a video report? Sent it to the station and put it on the internet?" Hadley asked, hoping she would say yes.

She didn't. "No. I'm going to do the report, like you said, with Pamela's help. And take it to our station here in St. Louis, despite the fact that they didn't support me on the effort. Without the media links.

"And then, I'm going to fly to SNN headquarters and offer up an exclusive follow up program for them. Only it will include the duplicity of the media with the DHS in trying to suppress the information, and in effect, allowing the country to fall to the terrorists actions."

Hadley's breath hissed inward through his teeth. "Crazy is right," he said. "But it is what you are going to do, with or without my help, aren't you?"

Kellie had tears in her eyes, but she nodded.

"Okay. Put it together. I'll arrange for the trip to SNN headquarters. I don't have many contacts in and around New York, but I do have a couple. I'll try to protect you the best I can."

"Oh, thank you, Hadley! I'm not sure I could do it without you." She was in his arms for a long time, trying to control her emotions.

Kellie finally stepped back and met his eyes again. "We'll get on the report. Have it ready for the station here. They can preview it if they want, and either accept it in full or reject it. The main things are the internet presentation and the one live on SNN."

"Okay," Hadley said. "You do what you need to, and I'll get something set up in New York."

EPILOGUE

It had taken some fast, persuasive talking, a look at the evidence, and a preview of the report, before the St. Louis station would air it, with a live follow up segment with Kellie.

The SNN airing of the report turned out to be simple, despite Carla's interference. Though Sally and June had been forced out, through Carla's machinations, and Hal had left voluntarily, fearing for his family, Justin was still there and had been working behind the scenes, trying to set up something to expose Carla.

Justin hadn't been successful, but he had the heads of the network receptive to seeing what Kellie had. Having seen the St. Louis report, no one bothered to ask to preview the piece after Kellie told them it was the same report. She would be doing a follow up with new information, hopefully with Carla.

That sold it to the producers. Carla was no longer the pleasant co-worker she'd appeared to be. Stiff and angry, she got herself ready for the live interview. She didn't bother to watch the airing of the revised report, having gone over the tape of the St. Louis broadcast with a fine tooth comb, looking for anything that might link her with the DHS.

When the piece began to air, Pamela, in an out of the way office, triggered the upload of the video to the internet. It would be running parallel to the studio broadcast.

So Carla was totally unprepared when Kellie, with a smile on her face, albeit a rather shark-like one, handed her the notes and memos that did link her with the DHS program.

She went ballistic on air, stomped off the set and disappeared for a few minutes. Justin had clued in another of the talking heads and he was ready to take over the interview, more than happy to take Carla down.

Kellie was in the middle of explaining the timeline of the things she'd done when Carla showed up on set again, this time with a pistol in her hand.

Hadley tried, but he was too late to prevent the three shots Carla took at Kellie. The first two missed completely, but the third caught Kellie in the left shoulder and she went down off the chair, behind the anchor desk.

Studio security was right behind Hadley when he tackled Carla and got the gun away from her. Another few minutes, with New York City police just arriving, several DHS agents showed up and began to arrest people at the station.

Worried about Kellie, Hadley had gone with the ambulance to the hospital. Justin called shortly after they arrived and Kellie went into surgery, catching Hadley walking restlessly in the waiting room.

"How is she? And it looks like DHS is taking on their own. One of them said something about seeing it on the internet. There were some agents in on the scheme here in the background and they got into a battle with the good DHS guys and NYPD when the new agents tried to arrest them."

"I won't know for a while. But the doctor taking her in said she would be fine. He didn't seem worried at all. She was just in a lot of pain. Man, I should have been quicker! Anyone else hurt?"

"Only two of the bad guys went down. Minor injuries. No deaths. None of the good guys. A small miracle.

"And as long as Kellie is going to be all right, Hadley, that's the main thing. She, with your help, has prevented a disaster that had the potential of killing literally billions of people."

"Yeah. It was Kellie all the way," Hadley said softly. He put away the phone when Justin was called away at the studio for something.

As soon as the doctor let Hadley in to see Kellie after her recovery from the minor surgery, he was at her bedside, apologizing profusely.

"Oh, Hadley! It played out all right. We won, didn't we?"

"Yes. We... You won. DHS looks like they are going to clean house and some news networks have already started internal investigations.

"A lot of people in Washington DC aren't talking much, but don't look too happy about things. But for the moment, this particular crisis, as bad as it is, seems to be contained."

Kellie smiled, sighed, closed her eyes, and relaxed. After a few moments, her right hand still in both of Hadley's, she opened her eyes and looked at Hadley. "You remember a couple of our conversations? I think that the time, when times comes, is here. Give me your pitch so I can say yes, and we can start making wedding and prep plans."

Hadley's eyes widened, but he recovered quickly. He bent down, gave Kellie a deep kiss and then went down on one knee. The time had definitely come.

End

THANK YOU FOR READING "WHEN THE TIME COMES"

By

Jerry D. Young

LIKE THIS BOOK?

See more great books at www.creativetexts.com

PLEASE LEAVE US A POSITIVE REVIEW AT

www.amazon.com

THANK YOU!

46946738R00071

Made in the USA
Middletown, DE
12 August 2017